MW01041422

MISSIONARY KIDS ON TREASURE WORLD PART 1

By DOUGLAS BELL

MISSIONARY KIDS ON TREASURE WORLD – PART 1

PROLOGUE

God has made so many other planets! Astronomers are those that look up and study outer space. They began finding planets around other stars in the 1990's.

Shortly after that, in the twenty-first century there was a great and wonderful discovery. People were able to travel to planets around far stars as easy as driving a car to a far city. Well, almost as easy.

Many people moved to these far worlds. At first hundreds, then thousands, then even millions.

Time passed. There were stories of worlds where no one had heard of God or even Jesus.

Missionaries went to these far worlds. One such missionary had failed in all his missions. His supporters gave him one last chance. It was on a world owned by eighteen greedy miners. Would they turn from treasure to God?

The missionary brought his three kids. And it was a good thing, too! The kids would make a wonderful discovery that would change everything.

But, oh, the trouble they'd get into!

3

Chapter 1 – Missionary Kids

"How can Father make a planet believe in Jesus?" Kevin asked. He was a little boy traveling with his family aboard a huge spaceship with lots of other passengers. He and his family would soon be dropped off on a distant world. Amazing adventures awaited him. And Kevin would make a great discovery.

However, it was the afternoon of the day he would cause more trouble than the spaceship had ever known.

His big sister, Sandy, frowned and rolled her eyes up. "Not the world itself; the people living there." She made that strange sound-of-frustration in her throat. Kevin had tried but could not. It must be a sound only girls could make. Sandy said more: "He has to reach the miners working there; and their families." She would be surprised to know how much Father would need her help.

Sandy put her hands on her hips. She looked up at Kevin. He was floating in the middle of the room; and blowing bright shiny bubbles, as usual. It was one of the rooms that didn't hold you to the floor. The huge spaceship they were aboard had many like it. It could carry lots of passengers, luggage, and cargo.

Sandy warned, "You better be good this time, Kevin. This is Father's last chance. If he can't convert these people, the Galactic Missionary Society won't let him try again. It was your fault he failed the last time!"

Kevin was used to his older sister and all her talk. And how it echoed loudly around the big, empty room! She was slender and tall for

4

her age, so she seemed to tower above him. He liked these rooms. Floating up here, he was high above her. He blew some bubbles at her. The ones that were close made a group. Stick! Stick! Stick! Some floated away. Sandy had lots of long, dark hair which always, somehow stayed up on top of her head in different stylish ways. Even here in this room, her hair was under complete control. Kevin could never figure this out.

"That's not true, Sandy!" came Nicky's voice from the hatchway. She had lighter skin and hair color than Sandy — Kevin did, too. Nicky's hair was not as long as Sandy's and always in some kind of braid, or two, or three, or even more. Kevin's hair was a rough short cut that grew messier with time, until Sandy cut it short again.

Nicky wasn't as slender as Sandy; probably because she spent so much time curled up reading books. It was good she was so smart. There were amazing and unexpected problems waiting for her on the new world.

Usually, she read from a small, modern book-reader. It wasn't a book itself. It was actually a computer shaped like a book. It folded out and displayed pages — even in the dark, in bed, under the covers, especially if it was a scary story. Nicky liked it most because it knew when to turn the pages by itself. Sandy didn't read much — except for the Bible. She always had to be doing something.

Nicky's sticking-boots made that ripping sound each time she took a step. The floor was rough. And the bottom of shoes had special fuzzy stuff. "You always blame Kevin. What would Father say?" Nicky knew this always got to Sandy, her older sister. She loved the trick of making Sandy hear Father's voice in her head. Plus, it always settled her down.

5

Kevin swung his arms a special way. This made his body turn until he could see Nicky. He grinned down at her. She was five years older but always kind to him. Sandy was thirteen, two years older than Nicky. Sandy was always so serious these days. But Kevin knew Sandy loved him. She'd always looked after him — after Mother went to heaven. He watched a bubble by itself float away and finally pop. He still missed Mother...

It was evening onboard the spaceship; just before the trouble started. Sandy had just set the table for dinner. It looked perfect, as usual. And the aroma was mouth-watering. Sandy worked hard at being an excellent cook.

All was quiet. Nicky sat cross-legged on the floor in a corner, enjoying her book-reader — as usual. She was reading about how to build spaceships. Sometimes, bright pictures on the book-reader's screen would light up her face with colors.

They were in their one-big-room. A hallway led to the bedrooms. A tall hatch across the room opened to the rest of the spaceship. It was a simple room, just like most of the other passengers had. Father was at his desk. He was reading the Bible and making notes. He was preparing for his new mission to be the first missionary on a newly found world called *Caesar*. They would arrive soon, and he was spending more and more time studying. Sandy knew it would be hard to get him over to the dinner table.

Sandy looked at the table with everything ready to eat. She was pleased. Father would sit at this end. She would sit at the other, where Mother used to sit; Nicky on one side and her little brother Kevin on the other. And Kevin was, as usual, missing. She asked Nicky. Nicky took a deep breath and began reciting all the places on the spaceship that Kevin liked to go.

Before she could finish, the spaceship began to shake. This had never happened, and Sandy's eyes got big and she sucked in her breath. Everything on the table now floated up in the air: the dishes, silvery utensils, and all the food! Nicky floated off the ground, looking around in curiosity. Father floated off his chair still reading the Bible so closely that he didn't notice right away.

Sandy stayed stuck to the floor because she wore the spaceship boots that stuck to the special fuzzy carpet. Something was wrong! There was no gravity to hold them or anything down.

The whole room began to sway and move in different directions. It became very noisy. Everything not connected to the floor or walls was now flying around, and crashing. The dinner Sandy had worked so hard to prepare splattered all over the wall and ceiling.

There was so much noise. Nicky cried out in fear and covered her face with her book-reader. Sandy reached toward her sister, but Nicky was too far away. Sandy crouched down into a ball. She wrapped her arms around her head to protect it from everything flying around. She, of course, began to pray. Father grabbed his desk, and his chair floated away. His body continued to swing upwards until he was upside down. He looked around, his eyes wide with alarm, and roared: "Where's our Kevin?!" Father forgot he needed to hold on to the desk and slapped his two hands together and began to loudly pray for Kevin and for the Lord to save them all.

Chapter 2 – Exploring

Kevin liked to blow bubbles and he liked to explore. Both were about to cause more trouble than he'd ever known. He was just six-and-a—half.

He was aboard a huge spaceship taking his family to some world far away. Kevin liked the rooms and hallways near the center of the ship. There wasn't as much of the stuff that held his feet to the floor. 'Gravity' is what his big, towering sister Sandy called it. She knew everything, for she was thirteen.

Kevin had even found a few rooms — places where they stored stuff strapped to the floor — where there wasn't any gravity at all. He'd enter, take off his stick-boots, and float off the floor.

He liked to blow bubbles in these rooms, because the bubbles did funny things. Some stuck together. Some floated off alone. The ones that floated off by themselves always popped. Out of loneliness, Kevin thought. It was so quiet that he could even hear the tiny sound of the bubbles popping. Tink! Tink!

The bubbles in groups stayed alive, floating all around the room until Kevin popped them. He could pop them by simply pressing a button at the bottom of his amazing bubble blowing bottle. If he didn't, then crewmen would find them, tell Father, and he'd be in trouble — especially if Sandy found out.

Today, he was going to explore a new room. It was far away from the rooms where everyone lived and ate and talked. Kevin walked along the dim hallway using his stick-boots. If he took them off in this hallway, he'd float off the floor for sure. He loved the ripping noise they made with every step.

In this part of the ship, there were lots of strange machine noises — humming and sometimes clanking. Nicky, his other big sister, knew how everything worked. She said this was where the engines were. Kevin couldn't remember what kind of engines. Nothing he'd ever heard of. Nicky would know how they worked if he asked her. Nicky always knew 'how', and Sandy always knew 'what.' And Father loved God and knew about Him. Kevin loved listening to Father talk about God. Mother used to — before she went to heaven. Kevin missed her and didn't want to think about it anymore. So, he looked ahead down the hall and started exploring faster. He loved to explore!

He heard voices ahead. Now he worried because of the ripping noise of his stick-boots. So, he took them off and stuffed them into his baggy pockets; he had pockets all over his pants. But before he floated up too much, he reached down and grabbed the fluffy rug stuff that covered the floor. He was able to pull himself along without making a sound. He moved fast this way, though it would be a little hard to stop.

Near the end of the hallway, he grabbed hold of the fluffy stuff and his body flipped over — his feet flying through the air — and wanted to keep going. He kept grabbing the fluff-stuff until he came to a stop. He twisted around and then peeked around the corner where he'd heard the voices. He saw a hatch closing on down at the end of that hallway. When it clanged shut, there were no more voices. He was alone here.

Right in front of him was the closed hatch he was dying to open. The day before, he'd been down following crewman Dan who was his friend. Crewman Dan said no kids were allowed past the door because this

9

was the Control Room. Dan pressed the buttons next to the hatch in a special way to get the hatch to unlock and open. Then he made Kevin wait outside while he went in to check the systems. Kevin was dying to explore the 'systems.' He didn't know what they were. Nicky said they made the ship and everyone in it slip through space faster than even light moved.

Kevin had a ring with a flashlight. But try as he might, he could never see how fast light moved out of it. It was just too fast and always appeared on the other wall faster than Kevin could turn his head to look. The ring had other wonderful powers. Father had given him the ring for Christmas.

Kevin remembered the buttons Dan had pressed. He looked around, and then floated over to the hatch. He touched its cold, metal surface. It was big! He pressed the buttons just like Dan. He heard a hum and some clicks. The great hatch before him began to slowly swing out. Suddenly Kevin felt tense. He wasn't supposed to go in here. He looked around and behind him down the hallway. Well, if he was careful and nobody found out, then he wouldn't be in trouble. If Sandy found out... He shook his head to clear the thought.

When the hatch was open enough, Kevin looked in. Wow! The room was dark but there were tiny lights of different colors all over the place, some blinking. And there were lots of display screens with strange shapes, different colors, and lots of words. Some of the words were moving. As he moved in further, the lights turned on by themselves. There were controls and buttons and levers all over the place.

But right in front of him, across the room, was a big square door with a big red button right next to it. Kevin pulled himself in using the fluff-stuff on the floor. He put his stick-boots back on. But they made that tearing noise with each step. It seemed loud in here. So, Kevin quietly closed the hatch behind, so no one would hear. He approached the big square door.

The button had a plastic cover on it. He lifted it and pressed. Lots of clicks. Then the door began sliding down into the floor! As it did, he heard a great, low humming ahead. And then he saw the most amazing sight. It was a big room the shape of the inside of a can. Strange, fuzzy-looking windows were everywhere on all the round sides. At the back end were all sorts of shiny metal parts. And there were really weird moving lights behind all the windows.

There was no place to walk. But between the windows was a narrow strip with hand rings. Kevin reached in, grabbed one, and pulled himself in. His stick-boots both made a loud 'rip' as his feet left the floor of the Control Room. There was nothing for them to stick to in here.

He pulled himself along until he was in the center. The room was very warm. He looked around and gulped. He was inside of a huge, shining can. He looked back at the open door. Good thing. He would hate to get trapped in here.

He looked at his hands in wonder. The weird lights from behind the windows made his hands light up with strange and slowly changing colors. "This would look great on the bubbles!" He always spoke out loud when he was by himself and he was nervous. This was a scary place. But he decided to be brave like his father. His father went to scary places to tell people about God. Sandy said Father was a missionary, and missionaries went to scary worlds to tell people about God. Kevin was proud that his father was always brave about this, even when things didn't work out right and they would have to leave — sometimes really fast.

Kevin pulled his bubble-bottle out from one of his big, baggy pockets. On the side of the bubble-bottle were knobs to turn, and control buttons to press. These told the bubble-bottle what kind of bubbles to blow, how big, what color, what shape, and how fast they came out. To begin with, Kevin set it for a great big clear bubble and pressed the 'GO' button. The top popped off to the side. Then a bubble began to slowly grow from the hole at the top of the bottle. It grew bigger and bigger and then floated free. It was bigger than Kevin's head!

He blew a few more big ones. The bubbles shined with colors — the same colors as the windows all around the strange room! He blinked and laughed out loud. And like his bubbles usually did, they drifted toward each other, slammed together, and stuck. Nicky had told him about how special the liquid was that she poured into the bottle. But Kevin couldn't remember all that she said. He had been too excited that day, his birthday, when he got the bubble-bottle.

He now pressed the control buttons and turned the knobs to make lots of bubbles of different small sizes. The bubble-bottle quickly blew out bubble after bubble, all shining brightly with the light from the amazing colored windows. Like always, most formed groups but some floated away alone.

Soon, the whole room was full of bubbles. Kevin was delighted and blew more and more. The dancing, colorful bubbles all around him made the most amazing sight he had ever seen.

But then he heard a strange hiss sound. He looked toward the end where all the shiny metal things were. There were rods and disks and other shapes he had never seen. Some of the bubbles drifting over there were bursting against the metal. They left a little bit of liquid. They always did if they hit something sharp enough or hot enough to make them pop. The liquid made the metal hiss. Kevin pulled himself closer to it. He could see the liquid sizzling like when Nicky tried to fry things in a skillet. Sandy would then have to help her. Sandy helped with everything since Mother had gone...

Sandy! Suddenly Kevin came to his senses. What in the world was he doing?! If he got caught here... A loud pop came from the metal equipment and frightened Kevin. He looked over and a round globe-thing was cracked and oozing a bright green sticky goop. There had been a large bubble near it a moment ago. It must have popped on it! He now heard a fan turn on somewhere nearby. All the bubbles in the room began drifting toward this end of the room. Kevin was horrified. As he watched, more and more bubbles burst all over the metal parts, causing all sorts of awful noises. A loud buzzer from outside the big, can-shaped window room started going off. Kevin began to shake, and he felt his heart beating in his head.

He let go of the bubble-bottle, which floated away, and quickly began pulling himself along the handholds to leave the window room. But there came a loud, crackling sound from behind him, and suddenly the whole room began to shake. And then it moved suddenly. The wall banged against Kevin and threw him toward the center. His hands were yanked from the hand rings and he floated out of reach, helpless. He twisted and turned and tried to grab back at a ring. Suddenly, he heard a loud warning siren out in the Control Room. Out loud he said, "Oh, no!" The door at the end was sliding closed.

Chapter 3 – Crisis

The poor spaceship was out amongst the stars. It was far, far, far away from any star with worlds that had human people. It was only a few days away from where they were going; a big, yellowish ball of a planet named *Caesar*. It went around and around a bright yellow star named *Rome*. But now, because of the trouble Kevin was causing, the spaceship wasn't moving at all.

Spaceships didn't move by pushing against something, like people and animals do when they walk or run. Or fish do when they swim. Or birds do when they push their wings against the air.

A rocket pushing against its fiery exhaust shooting out its tail end would be much too slow to get to another star. Stars were too far away! It would take that kind of rocket hundreds or thousands of years. The passengers would get much too impatient.

There was another way. The great, huge spaceship that Kevin, Nicky, Sandy, and Father were on — now shaking badly, as it was! — simply changed its location to get where it was going. But it changed its location very fast. Just a little bit at a time; just a tiny little bit called a quantum. But it did it very fast, and every single part, every single atom,[*] changed location at once.

To get a little closer to their destination world, the atoms of the spaceship were not *pushed* from their old location to the new location. Instead, their location was simply *changed*; a little bit at a time. This was

---

[*] Atoms are the tiny, tiny particles that all things are made of. They are too small to see, and a billion of them are in the period at the end of this sentence. Scientists have fun looking at atoms by using marvelous electron microscopes!

because the amazing engine of the spaceship sent out special forces. A magnet sends out forces to pull or push another magnet. And these weird forces were also vibrated a special way. And this made all the atoms of the spaceship suddenly feel like they were all in the next little location over. And feeling like you were just a quantum closer was the same as being there! But this is all taught in school so there's no need to go on...

So, a spaceship actually "shifted" from one world to another. It only took a few weeks to get to another planet around a far star. This method of space travel was invented by a famous scientist long, long ago from a town called Pleasantopia back on Earth.[*]

It was a very quiet way to travel. Everyone aboard the spaceship had their own rooms. And there was a large, common room with comfortable chairs. Here, passengers could watch the stars pass by on large display screens, so big they went from floor to ceiling. The stars did not move by very fast. There was no sound from outside. Just the sound of voices and the spaceship's engines which hummed a little; or sometimes made the funny noises Kevin was now hearing; trapped, as he was, in the engine room at the ship's center.

The poor spaceship was shaking badly. And the gravity, that held people down to the floor, was gone. Many of its passengers and crew had floated off the floor, and were bouncing off walls or floating things, and getting hurt. And it was anything but quiet. Frightened people were screaming. Things were loudly crashing together. The crew was shouting orders and instructions. And almost everyone was praying to God; on the

---

[*] Earth is the planet where all human beings came from, in case you the reader aren't from there.

inside or loudly crying out. Some prayed just a little, and some prayed on and on...

And the Lord heard their prayers and reached out to the tiny ship in the middle of black space all by itself...

The captain's strong, confidant voice came over the intercom all over the ship. She said some reassuring things to the passengers, and then gave sharp orders to the crew. An amazing calmness had come to her; an almost liquid feeling of peace. She had allowed herself only a short prayer because she had to deal with the crisis...

Kevin was still alone in the engine room. He had grabbed a handhold on the wall when the swaying ship had thrown him over there. Now he watched the weird colors behind the windows grow duller and duller, and then go dark. And now he was in complete darkness except for little lights at the end of the room, where the bubbles had done the damage. There were strange noises all around, and a terrible smell of awful burnt things. Kevin began to cry. He didn't want to. He wished someone else were here. He sure wished his mother could be here. This made him cry more and he bit his lip to make himself stop. What would Father do? Kevin thought of Jesus and began to pray to him. He prayed out loud as if Jesus was right there floating, too. He'd never heard his voice shake so much.

The captain of the spaceship had asked the spaceship's computer what was causing the trouble. The trusty computer had told her and her officers gathered in the command room all about the damage. They ordered the computer to turn off the engine, and this stopped the shaking. Next, the captain ordered the computer to connect her voice to the closest crewman to the engine room...

Crewman Dan was holding tightly to some strong, metal tubes that were connected to the wall. He was in a large, storage room, where he had been working when the spaceship began to shake. Now it had stopped. The little radio attached to the shoulder of his uniform gave out an important beep, and he heard the captain's voice giving him orders. He quickly pushed away from the metal tubes, floated to the door, and headed for the control room.

Kevin heard a noise beyond the door of the engine room. Then there was a clank and some whirring, a great hiss, and the door began to slide open. Lights came on, so bright that Kevin blinked. And there was crewman Dan looking in, his mouth open in surprise.

As Kevin crawled handhold to handhold toward the door, crewman Dan looked around, saw the damage at the other end, and whistled. He put his hands on his hips and looked down, as Kevin came to a stop and looked up. "Blowing bubbles again, Kevin?"

Kevin felt his face grow hot. All he could say was: "Please, Dan, don't tell my sister Sandy!"

But she found out. And Kevin was grounded — or 'floored' it should be called aboard a spaceship. He was actually locked in his room down the hall from their big room, where Sandy and Nicky and Father were cleaning up the mess. Everyone aboard the ship spent the next few days cleaning up and repairing damage. Many had been hurt, and the ship's doctor was kept busy. Everyone found out what Kevin had done, and many were quite angry. Poor Dan was in trouble with the captain for letting Kevin see the secret code for getting into the control room. She knew crewman Dan liked kids a lot and often showed them around the ship. Their parents liked this and complimented the captain on making life aboard ship easier. Dan had children of his own once; and a wife. But this was a long time ago back on his home world where there were many bad men, and bad men controlled everything. Something awful happened to his family that he didn't ever talk about. But he sure was happy to see and talk to the passengers' kids.

The captain decided she would just make him promise to be more careful around children, and to help repair Kevin's damage to the engine room. He did a great job, and the spaceship was ready to continue in just a few days.

And the world of the greedy miners — the missionary kids' new home — was its next stop.

Chapter 4 – Arrival

The day of arrival, Kevin was very excited. They had not allowed him to leave the family's rooms since the disaster. So, he was eager to explore something new. And it would be a whole planet!

The spaceship would not be landing on the planet. Nicky told Kevin that the spaceship never landed on a planet. It was only built for space and would be squished by a planet's gravity if it tried. They would be taking a small, shuttle boat down to the surface of the planet.

Only their family was landing here. The other passengers of the spaceship were on their way to other worlds. And, the owners of this planet, *Caesar,* did not allow tourists or visitors anyway. Kevin thought this odd and asked Nicky. Nicky shrugged and asked Sandy. The three were standing in their main room waiting for Father to return with a porter to take their luggage. It was now all packed and waiting near the big hatch that opened to the hallway.

Sandy cleared her throat and lifted her eyebrows, like she always did when an answer was going to be rather long: "The planet *Caesar* was discovered by the Christian Scouting Society. There's a chance that it has valuable minerals and gems. So, it was sold to a group of miners who think they'll get rich.

"As you know from Father's last job on that last world," Sandy paused for a dramatic shiver. "Whenever the Society sells a world, the people buying must promise a few things. And one of those things is that they must host a missionary or a pastor. If they don't, then they can't keep

19

the planet. These miners chose a missionary because they don't believe in Jesus...yet."

Nicky groaned. "They'll chase us away like the last place!"

Sandy waved a finger in the air. "No, no. Those people on the last world were the kind that only wants pleasure. These are miners. Father says they are quite behaved, though all they want to do is make money. This isn't good. But Father says their love of God will be all the stronger, once they believe."

Kevin asked: "Why don't they believe?"

Sandy blinked and suddenly could think of nothing to say.

Nicky put her hand on Kevin's shoulder. "They're probably from places where people haven't heard about the Lord yet."

Sandy finally responded, her brown eyes blazing: "They don't believe because they haven't heard Father yet!" No one had more confidence in Father.

Nicky grinned at her older sister's passion.

Kevin asked: "Are there any kids?"

Before either sister could answer, the hatch clanked open. Father stood in the hallway with his hands behind his back. Two porters loaded their luggage aboard a flat tractor and they all said good-bye to their little home aboard the spaceship.

On their way, they also said good-bye to the other passengers they had made friends with, and good-bye to the crew. Kevin looked up and had to say good-bye to his friend crewman Dan. He felt great tears fill his eyes. It felt like there was a hole in his chest. Dan had been holding his hands behind him. Now he brought them forward to give Kevin a parting gift that had been hidden behind his back. It was Kevin's bubble maker! Kevin hadn't even thought of it after leaving it behind in the engine room.

A hatchway slid open and they all stepped into a long room with lots of seats all in rows. They were told they were now in the shuttle boat! It was very comfortable. Soft music was playing. The steward even served candies and juice to them.

A big display screen stretched from floor to ceiling. It showed what was outside the spaceship. They saw black night with sharp, bright stars everywhere. And nearby was the planet *Caesar,* a great glowing ball, lit up by its sun, the star called *Rome.* The planet was mostly yellowish in color because it was completely covered by churning, swirling yellowish white clouds. It was completely covered, except for a thin, patchy strip that went all the way around its middle. This strip looked amazingly just like a ribbon with laurel leaves all along it.

There were fewer clouds over this patchy area. This was the only area of the entire planet where they could see between the clouds. They saw a mishmash of many dull colors: small areas of brown, dark red, dark green and dull yellow. There were a few areas of bright blue and light pink.

The pilot came over, pointed down at the planet, and told them about it. He explained that the patchy strip around the middle was where they were headed. That's where the mining colony was. It was the only area where anyone could live. The rest of the surface of the planet was all storms, all the time.

Kevin asked why they didn't fall down, on the planet. The pilot explained: The spaceship was actually moving around and around the planet. It moved fast enough so that it wouldn't fall down to the surface. Kevin looked down. It didn't look like they were moving at all.

A large long hatch opened out of the spaceship. Out floated the shuttle boat. Its rockets fired up at the back end. It went down toward the patchy strip around the middle of the planet.

Another object floated out of the spaceship. Rockets flared at the end of this object, and it moved in a different direction. Only Father knew about this.

The shuttle boat hovered high up in the sky. The pilot was radioing the town below for permission to land. The shutters of all the windows of the shuttle now opened letting the missionary family look out at their new world. To the north and south, they saw only dark gray along the edge of the world. This was where there were storms all the time. To the east and west, they saw areas of different dull colors as far as the eye could see. They were above the patchy strip that went all the way around the world. Above, there were fast moving gray clouds.

Below, they saw the town that would be their new home. It was the only town on the whole world.

It wasn't directly below them, but about a mile away. Right below them was the landing field for spacecraft. This kept the town safe in case a spacecraft blew up when it landed. This had once happened. Sometimes the miners of *Caesar* allowed space traders to come sell them supplies and also things that no one should ever really buy. Once, one of these space traders had landed his junky old looking spaceship and it had blown up. So, the miners kept the landing field far away from Town. They also shoveled up huge rings of dirt into hills around the landing field. So, if another ship ever blew up, the fiery blast would hit the dirt and not Town.

Town was small. There weren't more than one hundred people there. There was a big, square wall around the town to keep out dangerous creatures. At each corner of the town's wall, there was what was called a *photonic canon*. Each canon shot big blasts of photons.* If any spaceship ever tried to steal the miners' valuable gems and minerals, the canon would be used to blow them out of the sky. This had never been done. However, there was a way to practice.

Every now and then, the town trash masher was full. It then crushed the entire town's trash down to a thick, solid cube. Everyone would then come out to watch the *trash fling*. One of the miners, named Flart, was good at building mechanical things. He'd made a catapult big and strong enough for flinging the big, heavy trash cubes. The catapult was on a round platform that would turn, and they could fling a trash cube in any direction. This was all to test the canon. But the miners enjoyed it. The trash cube was thrown high into the sky and away. A miner would be in the canon control room at the town's meeting hall. Or he'd stand nearby with a remote control. He had control of the canon at the four corners of Town Wall. He would aim a canon, fire, and blow the trash cube to bits. They took turns doing this. If he missed, the next miner in line would quickly push him aside and take a shot before the trash cube fell to the ground. Any miner who did not behave day to day would lose his turn to shoot the trash. And the miners bet their treasure on who would hit or miss.

---

* Photons are the tiny bits of stuff that light is made of. They are much too tiny to see. But when you see a bunch at once, that's light!

The meeting hall was at the very center of Town. Only the miners were allowed there. There were eighteen of them and they all owned the planet *Caesar* together. There were some laws that all the planets shared. If the miners ever got caught breaking these laws, they would not own the planet anymore. Also, because the planet was found by the Christian Scouting Society, the miners had to host a missionary or pastor. This was part of the agreement when the Society sold the planet to the miners. But the world the miners were from had a bad reputation. And the miners had been on the planet *Caesar* for fifteen years with no missionary, pastor, or any Christian person at all — until now.* The missionary family were the first Christians to the world ever.

There was a ring of small, silvery dome-shaped buildings around the meeting hall; about a couple hundred feet away. These were actually the tops of huge, oval-shaped underground storage chambers. They were the most important buildings in Town, to the miners. In them, they stored the treasure they mined from all over the planet. The miners spent most of their time looking for, mining, and gathering valuable minerals, rare and precious gems. Each miner wanted to get rich enough to buy his very own planet. They had all put their money together to buy the planet *Caesar*. They were all supposed to work together and share all they found until there was enough for everyone to buy his own planet. Often, one would find a rich treasure trove. He'd be tempted to keep the location a secret and not share with the others. This caused big trouble.

The treasure they all found was supposed to be divided evenly back at the center of Town, in the meeting hall. Then each miner stored his

---

* It had taken the Galactic Missionary Society fifteen years to find a missionary brave enough. The people of the home world of the miners had a very bad reputation.

portion in his underground chamber. But the miners sometimes found ways of cheating each other.

Each miner had his own underground chamber that was locked up securely. Only that miner could get in. Sometimes, others would try. And this caused the biggest trouble. Nothing meant more to a miner than his hoard of treasure.

The meeting hall was at the center of Town. The tops of the underground storage chambers made a ring around it. And around that were the houses where everyone lived. They were all block-shaped and dull-white. There were no colors.

Beyond the houses, but still within the surrounding Town Wall, there were other buildings: The laundry, the clinic, the automatic shopping mall run by robots, the trash building near the catapult, and others. An automatic farm was in the northeast corner of Town. Still up in the shuttle boat, the missionary family could see shiny metal robots working the green farm area. The southeast corner was the town utility yard. It was surrounded by a wall to keep everyone out but the miners.

There was a large gate in the middle of each of the four sides of Town Wall. Each gate had a name. The gate in the middle of the north wall was called 'Farm Gate' because it was near the farm. The gate in the west wall was 'Laundry Gate' because it was near the laundry building. To the east was 'Trash Gate' because the trash catapult thrower was nearby. To the south was 'Port Gate' because it led to the landing field a mile to the south — the only space port on the whole world.

And this was where the shuttle boat was about to land.

There were always fast moving light gray clouds overhead. The clouds had looked yellowish when the boat had been above them. But they appeared gray, now that the boat was under them. Nicky was dying to find out why.

A thick cloud moved in front of the sun above and the whole town below became dark and gray. Sandy gulped and had a sudden feeling of great dread.

Nicky sensed her sister's feeling, and to cheer her up asked their father: "What's there to do there?"

Kevin interrupted: "Are there any kids??"

Their father gently got after Kevin for interrupting. They didn't know much more about the new world, because there was very little written about it. However, Father reminded them that it was a modern colony with lots to do even though it was small. They would all be going to school (Kevin groaned), and that it was a wonderful new planet with lots to explore.

When Kevin reacted with great excitement and began bouncing up and down on his seat, Father cautioned him to be very careful because a new planet could hold great unknown danger.

They waited a long time. Finally, the shuttle was given permission to land, and did just that. They watched with excitement. It moved down toward the middle of a large flat area. This was surrounded by two huge rings of shoveled up dirt, making it look like a bull's-eye from above. The shuttle rockets blew up a huge cloud of dust, which blew away, up and over the surrounding dirt hills.

MISSIONARY KIDS ON TREASURE WORLD – PART 1

The boat landed. The family said good-bye to the crew. Father recited a heartfelt blessing and they stepped into the little airlock room and the door closed behind them. The air of *Caesar* was okay to breathe, but the crew was not allowed to open the shuttle to the air of any world. Otherwise, microbes* might blow in that could hurt the boat or the spaceship. God had designed human bodies to easily get rid of microbes. So, the air of most worlds, like Earth, was safe for people.

The outside door opened out then down making a stairway. The outside air began blowing in with a mild breeze. It smelled good and fresh! The children looked at each other in excitement. Father began saying things from all over the Bible. He did this at the beginning of each mission. The children were used to it. Sandy listened to every word. Nicky tried, but she was very excited. Kevin was eager to get out and explore.

Their father raised his arms and began asking the Lord to bless the mission.

The three children also prayed — but secretly and silently in their heads. Sandy secretly prayed for the mission to be a success for her father. Nicky prayed that there be lots to learn about. And Kevin prayed for lots to explore. And God listened to their prayers.

They all stepped forth to the world that would be their new home.

---

* Microbes – tiny bugs, plants, or fungus too small to see.

Chapter 5 – Mr. Flan

They looked up and were amazed by the sky. It was not blue but a soft yellow, like the skin of a peach. There were clouds all over, moving rapidly.

They looked down. Kevin kicked at the ground, which was light brown dry dirt. They looked around but could only see the shuttle boat and the ring of surrounding dirt hills. Father told them someone was coming to pick them up.

Behind them was the big, white shuttle boat. Nicky reached out and touched its cold, hard surface. It had carried them down from the spaceship. The spaceship was so high up that it was even higher than the sky; up above the air of the planet, in outer space where there is no air; where they'd been traveling for weeks. They had not seen the shuttle boat since it had first picked them up and taken them aboard the spaceship.

It was as big as a flying bus. It had powerful engines sticking out. And they were still humming and giving out a little smoke.

There was a noise from the boat. The cargo bay opened up and several large, metal storage boxes were set out on the ground by robot arms.

Kevin excitedly ran off to explore. Sandy stayed with her father, and glanced up at the friendly, bright yellow sun high overhead. It was a yellowier yellow than the sun of Earth, the planet she was born on. It wasn't exactly straight above, so it must either be somewhat before noon or after noon. Sandy asked what time it was. Father didn't now.

Nicky had been watching the robot arms stacking the boxes, and their luggage. She turned. "I checked." She had spoken with the pilot of the shuttle boat. "It's two o'clock from noon. And there's forty-four hours in a day here."

Father and Sandy reacted with surprise.

Just then, they heard a humming sound from overhead. Over the dirt hills came a fly-car. It was fan-driven and raised a puff of dust when it landed. It had once been silvery, but was now dull, pitted and scratched up. The bubble-top was dark gray and part of it slid open. Out stepped a short, pudgy man of middle-age, bald but with some gray hair hanging around the back. He didn't exactly have a beard, but he hadn't shaved for a long time.

Their first miner!

He wore a buff-colored coverall and brown boots with really thick soles to make him taller. He blinked his small, bright eyes in the bright sunlight, then put his fists on his hips, and leaned forward, frowning at them. "So, you're the missionary?" His voice was gruff and a little high. "A 'man of God' so I've been told. You'll have to tell me about your God sometime..." Before Father could say anything, the man looked around, pointed to their luggage. "Well, grab your stuff. Robots aren't coming to pick *that* up." He went to the back of the fly-car and opened a storage compartment. "Put it in here. Hurry up, now! It's day sleep-time and I've been flying all day from working a far lode." They would learn that a 'lode' was what the miners called a place with lots more treasure than usual. He pointed to the compartment, poking his finger back and forth rapidly.

Father and Sandy went to get the luggage. Nicky hovered around them, sort of acting confused and helpless, to avoid having to help. Sandy stuck a box at her. "Here!"

Kevin ran back crying out in delight at the sight of the flying car. "Can I fly it? Can I fly it?"

The man moaned then said. "Three more kids! No, you can't, you young whelp! Hey, man-of-God, you don't have any *more* kids coming, do you?? How about a wife? You got a wife?"

Father told him there were only the three, and that he was a widower.

"No wife?? Well, you'll have to buy one like the rest of us. The trade ships that come by here sometimes have some women. Hope you got money. They charge a lot for ones worth keeping."

Father mumbled that wouldn't be necessary.

They finished storing their luggage. Father stuck out his hand and introduced himself properly. The miner grimaced with distaste, shook his hand loosely, and said simply: "I'm Flan."

All three children, well-taught by their father, said at once: "Pleased to meet you, Mr. Flan!"

Mr. Flan grunted, and then belched. Kevin burst out laughing at this. Sandy elbowed him to be quiet.

Another fly-car appeared. It was larger and louder and landed nearby, blowing dust all over them. It didn't have a bubble-top and was actually an open utility fly-truck for moving things. A robot was driving it.

Flan stamped over, waving his arms in irritation at all the dust. "Marty! You damned idiot! Parking farther from a fly-car is a higher priority than parking near cargo. I've programmed you that before!"

Marty the Robot was a cheap utility model; human-shaped but made of metal. He was colored a flat blue. He rotated his head to look at Flan, and his mouth display showed a big smile with lots of large white teeth. "Sorry, boss! Mr. Flatonicus told me yesterday to prioritize parking near cargo."

Flan stalked back to the fly-car grumbling: "...Flatonicus probably has got himself a secret lode..."

They heard Kevin's voice from inside the fly-car. "Wow, look at all these controls!"

Flan stuck his head in. "Don't touch nothing, you young whelp! Fly-car, lock your controls!"

The voice of the fly-car's computer calmly spoke: "Yes, sir."

They waited as Mr. Flan supervised Marty the Robot unloading outgoing cargo from the fly-truck. Marty then loaded all the storage containers from the shuttle boat into the fly-truck. Marty was extremely strong. Large, heavy support struts folded out of his legs and on to the ground, keeping him from falling over when he'd lift heavy things.

He then carried the outgoing packages over, handing them to the robot arms of the shuttle boat's cargo bay. They checked each package for anything bad before stowing it inside. The robot arms had X-ray scanners that could see every type of atom of each package. Up on the spaceship, a crewman sat in the command room. She was watching on a computer screen everything the scanners saw. If anything looked bad, or dangerous, or if the computer told her there were disease germs in a package, she would command the robot arms to leave the package on the ground. She whistled when she saw what was in one small package. A miner was sending back a little of his treasure because he was getting low on Galactic money...

Mr. Flan shouted at Marty the Robot, "You wait for us to fly off first!" He glanced at the missionary family and said: "We're going back to Town." He then belched loudly. Kevin burst out laughing from inside the fly-car.

The rest of them climbed aboard the fly-car.

With a loud whoosh, and dust blowing up all over, they lifted off upwards, watching the shuttle boat fall below.

Now above the hills of dirt, they could see the town and its wall in the distance. This was northward, Mr. Flan told them. In all directions there was just flat plain with mottled, dull colored patches. In the distances, it became just a brown-gray blur. There were no hills or mountains, except for the dirt ones around the landing field. But far to the north and far to the south there was a solid looking thin dark gray strip. It looked scary, like a storm far away. And it was!

But the horizon to the east and west looked normal, just a boundary between the fuzzy yellow sky and the distant brown-gray ground.

As they began flying toward Town, they heard a distant rumble. They turned and saw the shuttle boat lifting above the hills of dirt. Its powerful rockets were brightly burning, raising a big cloud of dust. They watched the shuttle rise high up. It grew tiny and disappeared into the clouds. This made Sandy feel tense and kind of alone. Nicky wondered again about the strange life they led; always going to strange worlds with strange people. The sight of the shuttle boat going away made Father think even harder about what he had to do: Bring these miners to God through the gospel of Jesus Christ. Would they even listen to him? If they did not, it would be his last mission.

Kevin grinned with excitement at being on a whole new world to explore.

Marty the Robot in the fly-truck followed them.

Chapter 6 – Town

On the short flight to town, Sandy listened with pride as Father right away began telling Mr. Flan about the Lord. But the miner soon held up a hand and said he was too tired to listen. Father asked gently what the miners knew about God. The miner told him that the only sure thing was treasure in your pocket. Nicky, eyes wide with surprise, glanced at Sandy. Sandy rolled up her eyes and made that funny sound at the back of her throat when she was mildly disgusted with things. Father looked a little sad.

Kevin stared out the bubble-top, which was clear when looking from the inside out. He was fascinated by the ground passing below. There were splotchy areas of many different dull colors. But he saw no plants or animals. And there were no people. The only objects he saw were a few rocks.

The miners were all from a different world far away; an awful world. It had a name too nasty to repeat. Hundreds of years before, people had first come to the miners' home world to colonize it. No one had brought a Bible. By the time the miners of *Caesar* were born, no one on their home planet had heard of Jesus. Space traders came now and then to buy and sell, but no missionary ever came to tell them the good news about Jesus. The modern worlds had forgotten about this world.

On their home world, the miners of *Caesar* were all from families that mined. Their fathers had sold what little they could find to the space traders, who paid them modern Galaxy money. The miner's fathers used this to purchase modern things – their planet was poor and rather primitive. And it was an awful place to be a girl or woman. They weren't treated well, at all. Sometimes they were even sold to the space traders that bought and sold people.

When the miners of *Caesar* were young, they spent all their time together as a gang. It was safer this way. They gave their gang a very nasty name. And they loved to listen to the stories of the space traders. The space traders often got drunk at the taverns. They told exciting stories about far away worlds.

Back then, the young miners had a gang boss named, Fodorvek. He decided they would save enough money and buy a planet for themselves, so they could leave their awful home world. They mined and stole and did awful things to make money and kept it all in a secret pile. Years went by; many years. The young miners grew up. Most became fathers, but they never spent any time with their children. And there wasn't anything like marriage on this world.

Finally, when some of the miners were starting to have gray hair, they had enough money to buy a world. But they only had enough money for a world from the Christian Scouting Society. Their worlds were cheaper because the buyer had to promise to make it a Christian world. To make sure, the Society required the buyer to host a missionary or pastor, forever. The miners didn't care about Christianity. They didn't even know what it was. But they bought a planet named *Caesar*, which went around a star named *Rome*.

Fodorvek had become very powerful, by then. He decided that he would be king of their new world. One day, a rickety old spaceship came to take them there. It didn't have much room. Only room for the miners and the living and mining supplies they had bought from space traders. There wasn't room for any of the women they spent time with. And not

35

one miner cared about bringing their children or their mothers. They were all cold-hearted by then and dreamed only of getting rich and each buying his very own world where he would be king.

Over the years, Fodorvek had done bad things and said bad things to all the other miners. By now, they hated him. However, they pretended to like him because Fodorvek kept the money. But now it had all been spent to buy the new world and all the supplies.

On the day the rickety old spaceship was ready to leave and take them all to *Caesar* for the first time, Fodorvek was not around. Some of the miners wanted to go, leaving him behind. Others were scared that Fodorvek would then come after them. He was dangerous when he was angry.

The eighteen miners did 'last belch'* to see who would go and get him from his hut. It was Flankenmetz. But he wouldn't go unless two other miners went with him. They went to Fodorvek's hut and found him. He would not be coming with them. He would not be going anywhere.

The three miners just shrugged and belched. On this awful world, they were used to such horrible sights.

Happily, they went back and told the other miners the good news: They would have no king! They all boarded the spaceship and moved to their new world: *Caesar*.

The miner Mr. Flan made the fly-car tilt up, and it began to slow down, like a horse being pulled up. They were right over Town. There

---

* Whoever made himself belch last, lost. This was how the miners liked to pick someone to do something. But they belched a lot for other reasons. Everyone on their home world belched a lot. It was the thing to do.

was the meeting hall in the center. It was surrounded by the ring of eighteen underground storage chambers. Around these were the miners' eighteen villas, each a little different than the next. And around the rest of Town were service buildings of different kinds here and there. The farm filled the land up to the northeast corner.

But were there any children? Kevin looked down at Town, and asked: "Where's the people?"

The miner was yawning. "They're in bed where they belong."

Sandy made the throat sound and said with disgust: "It's the middle of day!"

The miner only laughed a little and steered the fly-car toward one of the villas over near the farm.

Nicky said, "There's forty-four hours in a day here. So, we'll all have to get used to taking a long afternoon nap."

The miner belched in a way that sounded like he agreed.

They landed, and Mr. Flan ordered them to get out of his fly-car. They stepped onto the light-colored sandy ground and looked around. He was growing irritable. He opened the storage compartment and ordered them to take out their luggage. He didn't even help. Then he closed the fly-car, told it to lock itself, and trudged off toward his villa.

They looked around and there was no one else to be seen. The fly-truck with Marty was landing in the distance behind some far away buildings.

Sandy shouted after Mr. Flan: "Where do we go?!"

He ignored her.

Father then called out loudly in his booming preacher voice. All three children were startled and looked around in alarm. He reminded Mr. Flan that the miners had agreed to host them. If they did not, they'd have to give back the planet and lose all its treasures.

At that, Mr. Flan jerked to a stop and slowly turned. There was a sideways grin on his grizzled face. He looked back at them for a few moments, and then let out a short belch. He slowly pulled a small, black device from his pocket. Sandy, expecting the worst, stood in front of Nicky and Kevin, put her arms back and around, and began pushing them backwards.

But the miner spoke into the device. He put it away and called, "Robot's coming to take you to your...new home." He then bowed mockingly, and said, "Welcome to Town!" He turned and stumped into his villa.

They looked around. There wasn't a soul to see. Everyone slept in the afternoon because the morning, on *Caesar* had been eleven hours long. The afternoon was eleven hours, too.

Flan's villa was several box-shaped, dull-white structures attached or connected with large, dull-white tubes. A short walk away to the right was another villa. There was another to the left. They both had the same color and style as Flan's but were set up differently.

Above them, the pale-yellow sun shined, and light gray clouds moved quickly to the side in the fuzzy yellow sky. Kevin kicked at the rough sand at their feet. The ground was flat all around.

On the other side of them from Flan's villa, was the eastern side of the high town wall. It was the same color as the villas. There were small, mysterious splotches of different color here and there. In the middle of the wall, there was a metal section that went from top to bottom. This was a gate that could be opened, though rarely was. They would learn it was called Trash Gate because the town trash pit was nearby — one of the utility buildings just to the south of them. At the bottom of the gate, in the middle, there seemed to be a door, just as high as a man.

Kevin ran toward the door to try it. Sandy ordered him back, but he ignored her.

There were other buildings in the distance here and there. Everywhere, the wall could be seen behind everything. It was too high to see anything beyond, except the sky. To the south, they could no longer even see the high dirt hills around the landing field.

To the north, they heard noises and looked to see the farm being worked by special farming robots. Curious, Nicky took a few steps in this direction, but stopped, not wanting Sandy to get after her, too.

There was a slight breeze that never stopped. Strangely, it moved eastward, in the opposite direction as all the clouds above which always moved westward.

It wasn't cold or hot, and smelled just fine. That was nice, at least.

Suddenly, the closest building to the south made a loud gushing sound. This startled all of them, except Kevin. He was closely examining the door in the wall to figure out how to open it. But the gushing sound soon stopped.

Father made them wait a long time and they were growing bored. Finally, they heard a familiar vibrating sound and a fly-truck appeared. It landed away from them, with a big puff of dust. Out stepped Marty the Robot. He saluted and displayed a big smile. He went over and picked up their luggage all at once with arms that grew longer when needed. As he walked to the fly-truck, a side door swung open by itself. Marty entered and stowed the luggage. He said, "Come on! I'll take you to your new home. You'll love it. We just made it a few weeks ago."

As the other three piled in, Kevin reluctantly left the door in Trash Gate. He'd just *have* to figure out how to open it…

The fly-truck hummed loudly and with an exciting blast of air, lifted upward. It had no top, so it was more fun than Mr. Flan's fly-car — except for Sandy who shrank back in her seat and didn't look over the edge. Father and Nicky looked around Town with curiosity. They headed southwest but turned now and then, never flying directly over any building. A walled-in area that Marty called the utility yard passed to the side. There were many buildings of all sorts of fascinating shapes. Nicky was dying to learn their purpose. The utility yard also had stockpiles of equipment and supplies; and robots walking around. Meanwhile, Kevin watched Marty work the fly-truck's controls. Kevin's mouth hung open in fascination. It looked so easy!

They flew up to an enormous building shaped exactly like a cube. It was several stories tall like a big office building. And, it was as wide as it was high. It was dull white like the villas. Marty flew the fly-truck once around it in a circle. The villa had not one window. Marty landed the fly-truck in front of the north side, which had a door in the middle; at ground level, of course. The building towered above them! It was enormous. The missionary family thought it must be an apartment building. It was big enough for at least a dozen families.

The fly-truck door opened by itself again. There was not one other person in sight. Marty stepped out, turned, displayed his biggest smile yet, and swung out his arm toward the house until his arm was ten feet long. He called cheerily, "Your new home! You'll love it! And it's ever so efficient. And we robots got to design and build the whole thing!"

Sandy wrinkled her nose and asked, "How many other people live here?"

Marty answered, "No one. It's brand new, and it's all yours!"

He retracted his arm, marched up to the large door in the center of the building. It opened slowly outward by itself. Marty bowed and pointed his hands at the doorway. "Come in! Come in! Get to know your new home while I get your luggage."

The missionary family walked slowly toward their colossal villa towering above them.

What would it be like living in a house this big?

Chapter 7 – New House

Suddenly, from the ground next to them, there was a loud hiss. Everyone except Marty the Robot jumped back in surprise. A small crack could be seen in the ground, and air was blasting out of it — very smelly air. A great fountain of dust puffed up high above them. The hissing suddenly stopped, and the tall column of dust slowly blew away. The crack in the ground was gone — filled in by the dirt.

They all turned to Marty and asked at the same time what that was.

Marty's mouth display was a wide straight line. His shoulders moved up, then down. He said neither the robots nor the Great Computer knew what made the dust puffs happen. "The Great Computer has heard some of the miners talking about this. Some were sure it was ghosts under the ground. They called it ghost-gas. But they all began laughing and belching. We have learned this means they may not have been serious."

Their villa was very near the south length of the wall around Town. They were actually across from the door in the middle of the wall. It was called 'Port Gate' because it opened in the direction of the landing field to the south. This was the world's only space port. Town was the only town on the whole planet. Kevin noticed the small door at the bottom middle of the big gate. Port Gate looked just like Trash Gate. Kevin grinned at having a gate to the outside so close to home. As he watched, another dust puff erupted near the wall, sending up another fountain of sandy colored dust; and then right next to it, another; then another and another, all in a line. Kevin cried, "Ghost-gas!" and began laughing loudly. Sandy shushed him.

They watched the dust blowing high in the sky. Nicky took a step nearer to Father and held his arm with both of hers. Sandy stood fearlessly for a few moments. But then she took his other arm. Father asked Marty the Robot if the dust fountains were dangerous. Marty displayed his big smile again. He said not except for the hole while the dust was blowing. The ground was always hard again afterward. Then he displayed a mouth that was a zigzag line. He said slowly that the miners forbid the Great Computer from exploring the dust puffs.

Kevin looked around and asked where the Great Computer was.

Marty pointed toward the smaller wall around the big utility yard just a short walk east and told them the number of the building where the Great Computer lived.

Kevin smiled and said, "Tell the Great Computer 'Hello!'."

Marty paused then said, "The Great Computer also says 'Hello.' The other robots send their greetings, too."

Kevin looked around again. "I didn't hear anything."

Nicky rolled her eyes up then down. "Kevin, robots and computers all talk by radio or light beams. You can't hear it."

Kevin grumbled, "Well, I didn't know..." He looked around and saw no other robots. "Marty, where are the other robots?"

Marty replied, "During sleep-time, we're busy inside the miners' villas. You're lucky the miners let you have me right now. There're only a few of us. We clean their mining equipment. Other times, we're in the buildings, inspecting, cleaning, fixing..."

Sandy interrupted, "Let's go into the house!"

And they did just that.

Stepping in, they found themselves in an enormous room. Their mouths all dropped open at the amazing size of it. Before the children could say or do anything, Father had them all join hands for prayer. Kevin extended a hand toward Marty. Sandy slapped his hand down and growled, "It's just a robot, Kevin." But Kevin noticed that Marty displayed a rather sad frown.

Father recited appropriate scripture, and from the King James Version. He did that at very important times. Kevin frowned because he didn't always understand all the words and wished Father would use English. Father knew several versions of the Bible by heart. He had used the very expensive *memory pill* to learn them quickly. A rich lady on a faraway world had given him a supply of the pills for free a long time ago. Because he knew the Word perfectly, the Galactic Missionary Society always sent Father to hard missions on very far away worlds, like *Caesar*.

And now Marty brought in their luggage and began the tour of their huge new home.

They were in the biggest room Kevin could ever remember being in. It was as wide as the house itself. The ceiling was high overhead. It was bigger than the main hall of the last church they had attended before coming to *Caesar*.

Marty told them the house was five stories high. And, he would soon show them the other four floors above. Nicky began taking long, careful steps in a straight line.

Sandy looked around the enormous chamber. She made the sound at the back of her throat and pointed out: "There's nothing in this room."

It was true. There was no furniture, floor covering, or anything decorating the walls or ceiling. It was all dull-white, like the outside of the house. Kevin began running and jumped a few times. Father noticed that fortunately there was no echo either.

Nicky finished pacing off the room. She cried excitedly, "It's twenty-eight feet wide and one hundred long! And I think the ceiling must be twenty feet up!"

Sandy pointed out, "This room is big enough for a church service. The entire town could attend."

Father suddenly looked at her. His eyes twinkled, and he slowly grinned from ear to ear. However, he kept his thoughts to himself, as usual.

Nicky asked Marty, "This villa is all for us?"

Marty replied, "Yes, do you like it?"

"It's fine," Nicky answered quickly. "But why is it so big?"

"The miners told us to build it this big. Here, I'll show you…"

Marty's mouth disappeared. The display now acted like a television. It showed them a scene of a room full of middle-aged men. They heard the voices of the men talking and laughing. They were in a rowdy mood. They belched a lot, too. Each was holding a tumbler of some drink. There was a table of food. There was also a table with a large map on it. Several of the men were talking over it. They would point to somewhere on the map, and then begin bragging. Their clothes were all dusty and dirty, like they'd all just returned from…*mining!*

A robot voice asked, "Sirs, what should be the size of the new missionary villa?"

No one answered. They were all busy. The view looked around the room. It was the view from the eyes of the robot that had gone to ask the miners. The robot asked again. Still no answer. The robot asked once more.

One of the miners now yelled jokingly, "Make it big enough so they'll never come out!"

The other miners laughed loudly at this.

The TV display ended. Marty's smile returned. He said, "So, we did!"

The entry door now closed by itself. Marty said the Great Computer controlled the house, and they could tell it to do whatever they wanted. Nicky cried, "Great Computer, open the front door!" And it swung open.

"Does it lock?" Sandy asked.

Nicky raised both arms to the side dramatically. "Close and lock the front door, Great Computer!" The door swung closed, and there was a loud, satisfying click. Kevin went to try and push it open but could not. And there was no doorknob.

There were three doors in the wall across from the entry door. Marty led them to the door on the right. "Your office, sir!" It opened into another enormous room. And it was completely empty. He led them past the door in the middle to the door on the left. They asked about the middle door. Marty displayed a grin and said, "That's special! Let me show you the dining room first." The entry room they were in was so big that it took them a little while to walk all the way to the door at the left. They were excited at how grand the dining room must be.

The door opened to the dining room, another enormous room. It was as wide and high as the office but seemed a little shorter. Unfortunately, it was completely empty. Marty led them in. There was a door to the side and a special-looking door at the far end. Kevin raced ahead and shouted at the Great Computer to open the far door. It was actually two doors that both slid open sideways, disappearing into the wall. There was stuff in the far room!

They all finally caught up with Kevin there. Marty smiled, and pointed. "Your kitchen for preparing your fuel!"

Nicky looked at the robot and giggled.

Sandy marched into the kitchen. There were cooking machines and food storage units everywhere. The miners loved to eat, and all had fancy kitchens in their villas. The robots had found plenty of kitchen things from all the spare parts. Being so far away, the miners had bought plenty of spare parts for everything they used. Actually, the miners did not have too many things. They didn't like to spend their treasure. But the few things they did have, they wanted replaced as soon as they broke.

Sandy nodded with approval and announced to Father: "This will do."

Kevin yelled, "Let's go see that middle door in the entry room now!"

But Marty slid* to a side door in the dining room. And said it opened to the same place. This and the first door to the dining room were quite fancy. Kevin ran his hand over the frame which had carved pictures of grapes and vines. The doors had raised carved patterns of squares and buttons. But the doors and frames were all dull-white like everything else. Marty displayed a circle for his mouth and his two dark eye scanners stretched bigger. He pointed to the fancy door. "Do you like it?? Do you like it??"

Nicky answered, "It's beautiful, Marty."

Marty smiled and said, "We robots were so happy to design such a beautiful home for you all. The Great Computer answered our every question about what humans enjoy!"

"Marty," Nicky said, as she touched the frame around the door. "The frame and door should be the color of wood, not white."

"Okay," said Marty. "Let me find out how...oh, yes, of course! How silly of us robots. We didn't think to look." Both doors and their frames now changed color until they looked just like wood. "How's that?" he asked.

Nicky clapped her hands together. "Photochemical programmability! It looks great Marty."

Kevin didn't know what Nicky had just said. She often used very large words to describe how things worked. But he whooped: "Wow! Now make it purple. And make that one over there green...with yellow polka dots."

"Done and done!" cried Marty, always happy to obey humans.

---

* The robots all had wheels in their feet that they used when inside on flat floors.

Both doors changed to Kevin's desired colors.

Sandy made the throat sound. "Marty, change the colors back." They looked like wood again.

"SANDY!" howled Kevin.

Sandy raised her eyebrows high up. "We don't live in a circus, Kevin."

Father held up a hand and told Kevin he could color the door of his bedroom any color he wanted. That is, if they had bedrooms. Father asked the robot.

"Come with me!" Marty said with excitement.

The middle door of the dining room opened, and they all stepped through to see a breathtaking sight.

Chapter 8 – Garden

They now stood on a tiled walkway, about eight feet wide. It surrounded a beautiful garden that was rectangle shaped, twice as long as it was wide. The children ran to the low wall that went all the way around. Nicky and Sandy cried out in delight as they looked all around at the beautiful, flowery garden. The children gripped the handrail on top of the low wall. It was as slippery as ice. They leaned outward and looked up. The garden was at the center of the house and was open all the way up to the bright yellow sky above. And upwards, they could see the four floors of rooms above them. They had a giant, five story house all to themselves! In his excitement, Kevin leaned too far. His feet came off the ground and he began to fall forward. Sandy grabbed him and pulled him back.

They now smelled the scent of the blossoming flowers of blue, red, yellow, and violet. There were all sorts of plants; some tall with big, glossy dark green leaves; others small with lots of tiny leaves. And some plants with no flowers but leaves that had fancy lines of soft colors. Marty spoke proudly, "The farm robots did the garden! They'll take care of it for you, too. And the Great Computer tells your house when to water each plant."

Sandy looked up to the sky again. Then down at the garden. Then up and down a few more times. "This is the most beautiful garden..." She couldn't speak anymore. She'd never felt such emotion in her. It was like something inside her neck wouldn't let her speak.

"Are there bees?" asked Nicky.

"Yes," replied Marty seriously, his mouth a wide straight line. "The Great Computer says it knows of 238,980 words with B's. And it is observing a growth rate of about 2,500 new words per galactic year with B's, as reported by galactic mirror database linkup with each passing spaceship."

Kevin made a twisted-up face and looked at Marty sideways. The robot sounded crazy.

Nicky laughed out loud.

Kevin now ran along the tiled walkway all the way around to the other side and waved back at them from across the garden. He turned, told the Great Computer to open the door behind him, and yelled: "It's another door to Father's office!" He stepped in and commanded the room to be black. All the walls, floor, and ceiling turned black. And because the light had come from them, there was no more light at all. To the rest of the family, Kevin had disappeared in the darkness.

To Sandy, it looked like he had been swallowed by the pitch-black room. "Kevin, come out of there!" she yelled, and ran around to the other side. She told the Great Computer to make the room white again, it did, and there was Kevin standing with his arms crossed and grinning up at his big sister. From across the garden, Father burst out laughing loudly.

Nicky looked around. "Marty, how do we get to the other floors?"

"On with the tour!" cried Marty, pointing a finger upward. Sandy and Kevin walked back, angrily bumping in to each other a little.

"Now," spoke Marty. His mouth had a slight frown, and there was a moustache displayed above it. "Do you want to lift to the next floor up or climb stairs?"

They all looked around. There were no stairs to be seen. Or anything like an elevator or lift tube.

"Lift!" cried Kevin.

They all happened to be standing together. The floor tiles on both sides of them and between them and the garden, all tilted up by themselves, to make a safe little wall around them. "How cute!" said Nicky, folding her hands together in front of her with delight. "They're Smart-Tiles® with nuclear strong binding edges!"

Sandy scowled down at her. "How do you know all this stuff?"

"I study while you watch the story shows all the time," Nicky answered.

Sandy glanced at Father, worried he might ask which story shows.

But Father only reminded Nicky to spend time studying the Word of God regularly, as well. Nicky bowed her head sheepishly and said that she would.

The tiled floor and the little wall around them began going up, lifting them to the next floor. They watched the garden slowly drop downward as they went up. The lift tiles touching the walls slid upwards silently, connected to the wall by strong atomic forces. The movement was perfectly controlled by the Great Computer telling the Smart-Tile's control software what to do.

Directly above them, the ceiling tiles slid open to make a hole. They slid down the wall past everybody, down to replace the tiles that had been on the floor below. Everybody was lifted up through the large square hole in the ceiling. When the tiles of the little wall around them touched the ceiling, these tiles stopped rising. When everybody came to a stop, they looked down and it looked like just tiled floor again.

Kevin clapped his hands together. "That was great! Can it go faster??"

"Yes, actually eleven point six times faster," answered Marty. "This, the second floor, is the first bedroom floor. We built a bedroom floor for each of you. The miners ordered us to build a villa for four people."

They all marveled at the view down to the garden twenty feet below.

Behind them was the door to the room that was above the dining room. They entered. It was a giant bathroom, as big as the dining room plus the kitchen. Nicky began pacing it off. At the far end were the usual bathroom devices. Nicky reported that the bathroom was almost thirty feet wide and about seventy feet long. Bigger than most living rooms! It made them feel tiny. The children jokingly agreed that Sandy was probably the only one who could throw something from one end of the bathroom to the other. And Sandy had a good throwing arm.

The children began arguing over what the color should be until Father stopped them.

Marty told them the room across the hallway was the playroom. The children excitedly ran over to see it, hoping that it was full of toys. It was directly over Father's office below. And it was empty. Kevin was very disappointed.

Then they went to the great room that was above the big entry room to the house. It was just as big. Marty said proudly that it was the bedroom. But it was empty. Sandy made a very long and loud sound in her throat and said there was no bed. Marty the Robot said nothing.

Father put a hand on Sandy's shoulder and told her that he'd get beds for them.

They went out to the hallway to go to the next floor. Kevin asked for stairs this time. So, Marty told them how to order the Great Computer to make stairs. They watched in amazement as the floor tiles of the hallway began lifting up by themselves. Their edges connected to the wall and slid up along it. Some twisted until they were up and down; some twisted until flat. They made a stairway. Above, ceiling tiles slid down the side of the stairs to make a low wall on the side, so no one would slip off to the garden below. Everyone climbed up to the third floor.

It was exactly like the second floor: a huge empty bedroom, a big empty playroom, and a giant bathroom.

Using the tiled hallway to lift them, they went up to the fourth floor; and then the fifth. Now they stood in the hallway of the top floor of the house. They looked down at the garden eighty feet below. Sandy quickly stood back. It was too scary to look down. Nicky was fascinated. She looked up through the opening in the roof of the house. She could see plenty of sky here on the fifth floor. She watched the clouds moving. She could feel the breeze from outside on her face a little.

Kevin began leaning outward on the slippery handrail. Sandy quickly reached out and yanked him back. She scolded him. Sandy didn't think the wall that went around the great center opening down to the garden was high enough. To get her mind off the dizzying height, she told everyone: "This, the fifth floor will be Father's. Nicky, you get the next one down. Kevin, the one below that; the third floor. It's the middle one so we can keep an eye on you. And I shall have the second floor." She did not like heights, and actually wished she could have a bedroom on the ground floor. Kevin and Nicky grumbled a little over not getting the top floor.

Sandy turned to Marty the Robot, put her hands on her hips, and asked: "Why is there no furniture in this whole house??"

Marty turned to her and displayed a straight-line mouth. "The miners ordered us robots to build a villa."

Sandy waited but he said nothing more.

Nicky went over and laid a hand way up on Marty's arm. "They're robots, Sandy. They do exactly as they're told." Then she looked up at Marty. (He was tall, even for a robot.) "Build us some furniture, Marty."

Marty lifted his big, metal hands and began wringing them. "We cannot. There are no materials to build furniture. The miners buy their furniture as they need it, from space trader ships or the mall. You'll have to buy yours at the mall."

Sandy's head jerked around. *"Mall?!"*

Nicky jumped in front of Marty and looked up. *"Mall?!"*

"Yes," Marty answered. He displayed a smile. "The automatic mall is the closest building to your villa...that way." He pointed.

Sandy and Nicky looked at each other, their eyes growing wide with delight. They grinned from ear to ear and grabbed each other's hands. Kevin watched as his sisters began hopping up and down, saying "There's a mall! There's a mall!" over and over again. He grew bored and went back to staring over the handrail at the garden, so amazingly far below. He pulled his bubble-bottle from his pocket and began blowing bubbles. He watched some of them blow up and out of the house through the great hole in the roof above. He watched some blow spiraling downward in the direction of the garden far below. He leaned out more and more watching the huge center open area fill with his bubbles. They were moving up and down, and spiraling around and around…

Sandy suddenly grew serious and turned to Father to ask if they had money. Father smiled and assured her that the Galactic Missionary Society had supplied him with enough to set things up.

Excited again, Sandy ordered the Great Computer to make a stairway down. She and Nicky wanted to go shopping right away. They all went down the stairs. Sandy was impatient and quickly ordered more stairs down to the next floor. Suddenly, she looked around and asked where Kevin was. She looked up the stairs and gasped with fright. There, two floors up, at the top of the stairs, they all saw Kevin's feet fly up as he began falling over the handrail. And the fifth floor was a deadly eighty feet above ground!

Sandy began running up the stairs. Father and Nicky looked over, not knowing what was upsetting Sandy. Then they all heard Kevin's frightful scream.

Kevin was falling off! And there was nothing they could do. Sandy panicked and tripped on the stairs, falling to her knees. Nicky stood in shock, feeling everything slowing down. She didn't know what to do. Father's quick mind, realizing they were helpless, turned to God and began praying for his son as hard as he could.

But there was someone else who could think really fast. And he had long arms, too. Marty the Robot, in his computer brain, made a call to the Great Computer and explained all the details of the current emergency.

MISSIONARY KIDS ON TREASURE WORLD – PART 1

The Great Computer played back the whole time the robot had been with the new family. The Great Computer listened to the playback of Kevin's scream. Ah! The Great Computer was able to calculate Kevin's exact location from the phasing of the sound Marty heard with his precise robot ears. Now, the Great Computer knew a lot about science; everything his builders could get. He knew exactly how fast Kevin was falling, because everything fell faster and faster the same way; except small, fluffy things, which fell slower.

The Great Computer thought ahead. If Kevin continued to fall, going faster and faster... The Great Computer suddenly realized the danger Kevin was in. The computer's brain went into emergency mode and increased all its electricity to maximum, so it could think fastest. It gave Marty orders.

Nicky was observing amazing sights. Sandy was on her knees, scrambling up the stairs. Father's eyes were tightly shut. She was near the wall and began to see something moving downward out in the open area; the garden was so far below. And she also saw Marty the Robot whirling around, his robot arms shooting out, extending out and out. His great legs unfolded so fast that when the supports hit the tiles, they made a loud noise. The object moving out in the open area was making a loud noise, too; screaming. It was Kevin. Her brother. Falling! Everything was suddenly growing very bright for Nicky.

Kevin felt two strong things grab him tightly on his sides. He came to a stop. And the two strong things, Marty's arms, he realized, pulled him in to the safety of the hallway. He quickly hid his bubble-bottle in his pocket because he knew he was about to be in big trouble again. He looked up at Father. But when Father opened his eyes, they filled with tears, and Father wrapped his warm, soft loving arms around Kevin. Father thanked and praised the Lord over and over.

Sandy came down the stairs, turned bright red, and began hopping up and down in anger, ordering Kevin to be more careful. Nicky went over to Marty, thanked him, and began talking about how slippery the handrail was. She found that it could be changed immediately. She told Marty to tell the Great Computer to change all the handrails of their house, on every floor, to be sticky.

When they finally settled down, they all went to see what was at the automatic mall next door.

Chapter 9 – Automatic Mall

As before, they saw no one outside. As they walked west from their villa to the automatic mall, they could see to the north the other villas and other buildings of Town, but no people. Marty the robot had told them that during the afternoon everyone was asleep. He called it 'day sleep-time.' They'd wake up at evening. At midnight, everyone would go back to sleep again for 'night sleep-time.' People slept twice each day because each day was forty-four hours.

The missionary kids wondered about the people of Town. The kids were eager for the evening when everyone would wake up. What would the people be like? They asked Father, but he didn't know. Why had only one person picked them up at the landing field? Would the people come to their house to meet them?

Their gigantic home rose high behind them. Ahead lay the mall. They were facing its end, which was very fancy and appealing. Nicky ran out to the side, so she could see how long it was. And the automatic mall was quite long! Nicky and Sandy were excited about how many stores must be in it. And plenty of children their age, as well! Kevin trudged along growing bored. And he felt bad because Sandy was still mad at him. He wished he could fly.

The mall opened automatically for them and a great, booming voice welcomed them. There was a great aisle all down the center, from end to end with chairs and tables and cheap sculptures here and there. High above, there were skylights in the ceiling and pictures of exotic, far away worlds. There were also beautiful decorations hanging from the ceiling. They moved, swirling and swinging, all flashing different colors. Exciting music began to play. On each side of the aisle was a long row of stores, all automatic or run by robots. The children grew very excited; even Kevin. Father wrinkled his brow in mild disapproval. But they needed to purchase many things.

Marty went with them. Everyone else in Town was asleep so he had no orders to do anything.

First, to the furniture store to purchase beds, chairs, tables, and other items. Then, there was a food store to stock their kitchen. And other stores for other household items. And Father let them buy fun things, too.

When they were done, Marty called other robots. They all looked mostly like Marty, though each was a different color. The miners had bought them all from the same company, so they could easily fix each other. Some were bigger, some smaller. They used fly-trucks to bring all the new stuff from the outside loading doors of the mall to the villa. The robots carried everything in and put it everywhere Sandy directed. Sandy loved directing things.

Nicky had a small computer strapped to her wrist. She could now talk with the Great Computer anywhere. She asked many questions. She learned more and more about Town and their new world. It showed her all sorts of pictures on the little display of the wrist computer. She also learned she could instruct the Great Computer to watch the inside of their house, and make a loud noise if Kevin leaned over a high railing again. Kevin tried it once. The noise was like an awful siren. He jerked back and never tried again.

Kevin wandered around. He found himself in his bedroom on the third floor. He crawled onto his new bed to try it out. He then found he was quite sleepy and fell asleep.

The others began to feel sleepy. It was about the same time now as nighttime had been on the spaceship. Father made sure all the robots had left. He then ordered the Great Computer to lock the front door. They all said goodnight. Except Kevin, who was already asleep. Nicky knew this. Her wrist computer showed her a picture of him sleeping in his room.

Nicky curled up in her big, comfy new bed. She thought sleepily about meeting the people of Town. What would they be like? She fell asleep.

Chapter 10 – People

Sandy heard the loud noise. She was the only one. Nicky and Kevin both slept with their doors closed. Father left his open, but nothing woke him up, except his loud electrical alarm.

She realized it was pounding. She told the Great Computer to turn on the light walls. She blinked in amazement at the size of her new bedroom. The other end was so far away that she couldn't even throw anything that far. She smiled, remembering how small the cottage was that they lived in at the last world. The pounding started again. She dressed quickly and went to see.

Out in the dark hallway, Sandy hesitated. She was *not* going to go open the front door by herself. She looked past the handrail. It was so dark! It was nighttime on the new world. She looked down. The garden in the gloom below had tiny lights all around, making it glow beautifully. The lights were slowly changing colors! Sandy looked up...and gasped.

She looked all the way up the great open space at the middle of the house. She could just barely see the handrails of the other floors above. Each went around making a rectangle ring. All the way up at the top it was open to the night sky. And what a night sky it was! The clouds were all still moving like in the day. But now, at night, they were all glowing with pastel color: green, blue, yellow, orange, and pink; some even mixing together. Behind the clouds, instead of black night sky with stars, it was shimmering gray. She could see no stars.

More pounding. Sandy told the Great Computer to make stairs all the way up to Father's floor. Up she went. When she got to Father's bedroom, she was breathing hard. She shook him, but that didn't wake him up. So, she did something that Father told her never to do — unless it was an emergency. She pressed the WAKE-UP button on his electrical alarm. *That* woke him up.

Sandy went to get Nicky and Kevin while Father dressed. They woke up easily and dressed. They'd slept a long time, and it felt like morning.

They all waited down at the front door for Father. Kevin wanted to open it, but Sandy made him wait. Father arrived, wearing fine clothes, and carrying his medium-sized Bible with 'HOLY BIBLE' in bright, gold letters. They told the door to open.

They looked out into the darkness. There was nobody there! Then they looked up and were amazed at the nighttime gray sky and all the clouds of glowing colors moving across. Town was a mysterious twilight from this. The sun had set long ago.

Then they heard a snicker. Kevin poked his head out and looked to the side. "Kids!" he cried.

Several children stepped out in front of the doorway. They were thin and pale. All wore the same loose-fitting floppy clothing, all light gray in color. The oldest was a boy about Sandy's age. The others seemed the same age or younger than Nicky.

Sandy stood forth. "Greetings!" she spoke with great seriousness. "Do you speak this language?" She used the common language of the Galaxy, though Sandy knew others. She picked up languages easily.

"Hey, you talk funny!" said one of the children. Some of them began talking among themselves, commenting on the new strangers in the big new house. Their accent, to Sandy, seemed rather muddled.

Sandy raised a hand for their attention. "Do you know Jesus?" she asked. Sandy was very tense and excited. This was the moment she would begin working with her father to bring these people to Jesus!

One of the children replied: "No. Is that him standing behind you??"

Sandy's eyes grew suddenly wide as she imagined that Jesus had come at last. Father said over and over that he could come at any time. Sandy jerked her head around to look. But it was only her family. Father was smiling. He winked at her. She hated when he did that. She was trying to be serious.

Father invited the children in, but they suddenly looked afraid and wouldn't come in. The oldest boy stepped forward boldly, as if he might enter. But he hesitated, looked behind him, looked down and murmured, "Our fathers told us to stay away." He looked behind him again, as if suddenly worried about something.

In the distance, outside lights were on at all the villas. And other people could be seen moving around. They heard male voices laughing, and some hooting.

The boy said seriously, "It's party-time."

Kevin grinned and cried, "A party?!"

The boy said, "Men are at the Meeting House. You better stay away. They're drinking heavy tonight."

Sandy looked up at Father. Sure enough, there was that hard look. Father did not approve of drinking.

Nicky spoke: "It's a long night on this planet. How late do you stay up?"

The boy shrugged and answered, "We do stuff for about half, then it's night sleep-time. After, the men go mining in the morning. Some go out now sometimes. Until they see the ghosts. Then they all don't go out for a long while."

"Ghosts??" Sandy, Nicky, and Kevin all said at the same time.

The boy slowly smiled mischievously. He had sandy blond hair, kind of messy. And he never opened his eyes enough for anyone to see what color they were. "Ghosts are out there. They come in the night. They say there used to be more miners, but the ghosts got them back before any of us remember. Don't go out in the night!" He grinned a little.

Sandy and Nicky felt the hair on the back of their necks standing up. Kevin slapped his hands together. "Ghosts! Let's go see the ghosts right now!" And he jumped out of the house and ran around to the side, heading for the door in Port Gate. Sandy and Nicky chased after him, squawking loudly at him to stop. The other children ran after. Father, with the Word of God tucked under his arm, marched toward the meeting hall.

Kevin got to Port Gate first. He tugged on the handle of the door, but the door was locked. He didn't know how to work the lock. Sandy, Nicky, and the other children arrived. Sandy wanted them to go back to the house. Kevin asked how to unlock the door. The other children didn't know. Kevin asked didn't they ever watch the miners do it. The older boy, named Fanson, said the miners never used the doors anymore. He remembered that they used to, long ago, when he was little. But that was back when they drove the sand buggies. After they bought fly-cars, they stopped using the sand buggies altogether. The boy pointed eastward to a shelter over between the wall and the utility yard. "That's where the old sand buggies are. Want to see them?"

Kevin and Nicky both said "Yes!" with delight. The other children led them over. Sandy followed, though she thought to herself they should probably go back to the house.

The buggies were all sizes. Some were closed cabins; and some open. All had lots of big, fat tires. They were all a light gray in the dim light. And very dirty.

They were fun to sit in, with thick, comfortable seats. All had large storage racks in the back. But none of the children knew how to work the controls or start them.

It grew too dark under the shelter to play around the buggies anymore. The children asked Kevin, Nicky, and Sandy if they wanted to see the rest of Town. Sandy refused and began walking home. But when Nicky and Kevin ran off excitedly with the other children, Sandy changed her mind and followed. She even began running and felt strongly excited, too.

They spent the rest of party-time, as they called the first half of nighttime, exploring all over. And they began to meet the other people; but none of the miners, who were all at the meeting hall. The other children stayed away from there.

Sandy began trying to tell the other children the good news about Jesus. But most of them ignored her as if they weren't hearing. Others kept asking what her words meant. It was frustrating for Sandy because they knew so little. They'd never heard of anything! Prayer, the home world Earth, love, joy, peace...nothing. They even asked her what 'God' was! She took a deep breath and knew this would take time. She would keep trying no matter what; Father would.

The three newcomers saw some of the mothers of the other children. They stood in groups quietly talking. They wore modest, loose blouses, dresses, and simple slippers. Some wore hats. Their hair was bound up. Sandy noticed these women wore no make-up, though it was available in the mall. The women became silent when the three new children were led over by the town's children. Their mothers just stared at the newcomers. Their faces were pale and cold in the nighttime twilight.

The other children pointed out each of their own homes and what was special about how it was built; how this house had a slanted roof; how that house had a roof that bulged up; how this house had a room with more than one window; how another had no windows at all...

Strangely, the other children did not invite Sandy, Nicky, or Kevin into any of their homes. When Kevin asked about what it was like inside, the other children wouldn't say much.

The houses were roughly arranged in a large ring. Inside this, the children pointed out the dome-shaped tops of their fathers' gigantic underground chambers for storing treasure. The children spoke in whispers about these. They bragged about how much treasure each of their fathers had; and argued over who had the most. Two fell to the ground fighting about it. Fanson, the oldest, brushed the hair out of his eyes and just watched with a grin.

The children wouldn't go beyond the houses toward the treasure chambers — not during party-time with the miners loudly carrying on at the meeting hall in the center. Sandy was glad Father was back safely at home — or so she thought.

More of the other children would join them. But then others would grow bored and drift away. They saw more and more of Town. The robot farm was eerie in the nighttime twilight. The great robot tenders and harvesters looked like slow-moving monsters. Now and then, one would move to the processing building. The farm store was in front of the processing building. The children went to this next. The lights automatically came on. Sandy and Nicky filled sacks with fresh fruits and vegetables that were already cleaned and shucked. And it was all free!

At midnight, a strange, low hooting sound began. It was a signal. The children explained it was time for night-sleep and turned for their homes without even saying "good-night." Nicky commented to her brother and sister that the children reminded her of some robots she'd met on other worlds.

The miners kept strict time schedules. They spent as much time every day mining as they could. They wanted to mine enough treasure to each buy his own world and be king. And they'd also heard of certain worlds where you could buy drugs that let you live forever without aging. However, these drugs cost a fortune. But, so what! They believed their world *Caesar* would give them all the treasure they wanted. They often argued over how much was enough. There were rumors that some of the underground treasure chambers were almost full...

Father arrived back at the front door to their huge, square house at the same time as the children. Sandy and Nicky saw that his hair was messed up. His big jaw was set, and his mouth was a straight line. He declared that he would be fasting all day tomorrow. Sandy and Nicky looked at each other and blinked. They knew something must have gone wrong. They also knew Father would be pleased if they joined him in fasting. Sandy was good at it. She loved the Lord and enjoyed holding fast to Him. Father didn't expect her to do this often, because she was so young. Nicky was good at pretending to fast. Kevin didn't understand any of this. His favorite thing God made was food, and he was usually the first to pray thanks when they ate.

They carried the sacks of fresh farm food into their new home, and then closed and locked the door for the rest of the night.

All went to bed without eating anything because they were fasting. Even Kevin said he would fast. Later, Father's loud snoring could be heard throughout the house, because he always left his bedroom door open. Nicky crept down to the kitchen door. Kevin arrived, too. They quietly went in and closed the door behind them. They giggled together. Nicky figured out how all the food machines worked, and then made them snacks. They prayed to the Lord, thanked Him for the food, and asked Him to bless Father's mission.

Would their prayer be answered?

Chapter 11 – First Morning

In the morning began the first amazing full day on the new world for the missionary kids.

It was a typical day. For the miners, everything was all about treasure. And they could just pick it off the ground!

There were loud vibration sounds as all the miners' fly-trucks took off. They flew off in different directions in search of the day's treasure. Most of the miners had fancy vehicles with a covered cabin in front that seated two, sometimes four. There was an open truck bed in the back for cargo and equipment.

Sometimes a miner would have a robot come with him in a utility fly-truck. This was usually when the miner needed help opening up a new mine deep into the ground. But this was rare. They were afraid of the underground. And, the other miners didn't like anyone getting too much help from a robot. He'd get more treasure than the others. They could have purchased more robots; one for each miner. But the miners didn't trust robots all that much. They didn't want as many robots as them.

Most of the mining was on the ground. And the miners searched the ground only around the very middle of the planet *Caesar*. They couldn't go too far north or south because great, dry storms blew there that were too dangerous to fly in. But around the very middle of the planet, it was mostly always calm. The breeze near the ground always blew to the east. The clouds high overhead always moved to the west.

The planet had no oceans or lakes or any water on the surface. There was water in the air. Town had large condensers in the utility yard

69

that took water out of the air and piped it to all the homes. The robots had built the missionary house next to the utility yard, so, they'd use as little pipe and wires as possible. There were spare parts and supplies for almost everything, but not a lot.

Most of the planet at the middle was flat ground. There were some hills that bulged up. There were a few mountains that looked like someone pushed up gigantic black rocks from deep underground. Over most of the flat ground, there was something that looked like moss of different colors. When the moss was peeled up, sometimes very special stuff was found. Sometimes it was powdery. Sometimes it looked like ice crystals of different colors. Sometimes it looked like rocks and round pebbles. The miners would carefully harvest this stuff into special glass or plastic containers. They had to use very special gloves; and sometimes special tweezers. And sometimes even magnetic ones. These could pick stuff up without even touching it. There was a tiny computer in the handle.

Most of all, the miners had to be careful not to touch the moss. Some had, when they all first arrived at *Caesar*. And now, some of their fingers were gone. The moss wasn't like any fungus or plant anywhere else. It sucked in a little air. Then it changed the tiny, tiny atom particles that the air was made of. The moss changed some into the kinds of atoms that the moss itself was made of. Sometimes the moss made mistakes when it was changing the atoms of air. It's not like the moss was smart or anything. It had no brains! So, the moss often made mistakes and changed air atoms into atoms of stuff the moss couldn't use. It would kind of 'spit out' this stuff. It left it underneath in the dirt. And the miners would come along looking for it.

People on other worlds would pay lots of money for certain kinds of this special stuff. It was very valuable. It was used to make all sorts of valuable things on many worlds. But to make the special stuff on other worlds was very hard. It cost a lot of money. And the miners could just pick it off the ground here.

So, of course, the miners tried to keep their planet a secret. They had special radios aboard little satellite ships. These floated way up in black space and went around the planet. They could warn a spaceship not to land — or else. The little robot satellite ships could warn the miners if there was an intruder. Space pirates were intruders. Then the miners would have to mount one or more of Town's photonic canon on fly-trucks. And they'd go hunt them down.

Trading ships were allowed to land at the landing field south of Town. If ever there was trouble, the miners were well armed with Town's four mighty canon. Trading ships brought food and products for the automatic mall, and sometimes other supplies and equipment. But it cost a lot of money to have things shipped all the way to the planet *Caesar*. So, the miners bought as little as possible. They were saving their treasure to buy their own worlds and drugs to make them live forever. Their families weren't given much. It was sad for their families.

After the miners had all flown off in search of treasure, their wives and children could relax and begin daily activities. The miners liked to eat. They expected their wives to have delicious meals ready when they came home. So, the women of the town spent much time at this. They'd usually gather in groups to visit the farm and meat stores near the robot farm. Next to the farm, on the west, was the farm store. It was in front of the large farm processing building. It had fruit, vegetables, and grains — all free

71

because the miners owned the farm. Some of the produce from the farm processing building went to the meat factory. This was a building connected to the west end of the farm processing building. It made meat and dairy products without using any animals. There were large tanks and vats. Robots kept it all working. The meat store was at the front end of the meat factory. Sometimes, a wife would purchase special food at the automatic mall. But this was expensive. She only did it when ordered.

There were other regular things to do. The children helped with some. Trash had to be taken to the trasher next to the trash catapult near the eastern wall. The miners had decided not to install an underground trash moving system. It would have cost too much. Their wives and children could do it for free. The same with the laundry. Instead of installing laundry machines in every villa, the miners had built a building for doing laundry. It had robotic machines that did laundry. It was near the middle of the western wall. The nearby gate in the wall was named: Laundry Gate. The wives enjoyed meeting together at the laundry every day.

And there was Town School.

The miners had put in a school, so their children would be smart enough to help them run the planets they would buy someday. At first, the wives were not allowed to learn anything at the school. The school was run by the Great Computer and could teach almost anything. But few of the children would go. There was no teacher to make them. It was more fun to play outside. So, the miners grudgingly let the wives enter the school — but only to teach, and not learn!

Father was still fasting that first day. He announced they would not eat until noon. He would be praying for his mission all morning. He was about to let the three children go explore Town when the Great Computer's voice spoke out. They looked around. The voice was coming from the wall, it seemed. The Great Computer was announcing that school would be starting soon. So off to school went the three missionary kids.

At the middle of morning, they marched for home to go eat. They were very hungry! Kevin began complaining loudly. Sandy began to get angry at him. But Nicky put a gentle hand on Sandy's arm and said, "What would father say??" This always settled her down. They hurried home to eat brunch.

But it was still the fast. They had forgotten. Sandy decided to keep fasting, like Father. She went off to her bedroom to pray, before returning to school. Nicky said she would wait until noon to eat. She really wanted to eat and was only fasting to please Father. Kevin ate like a horse and stashed a few things in his big pockets for Nicky later. Back they went to school. When Sandy wasn't looking, Kevin slipped a few things over to Nicky. She grinned with newfound appreciation for her little brother.

At noon, a sound arose louder and louder — the vibration of the miners' flying vehicles returning home. They would be hungry. There was a flurry all over town as wives rushed home. Each miner landed beside the dome-top to his underground treasure chamber. Each unloaded his day's treasure. He made sure his chamber was securely locked. Each went home to a big lunch. After that, they slept during the long day sleep-time all afternoon.

The missionary kids went home from school at noon. They found themselves quite sleepy, even though the sun was high overhead. But morning on *Caesar* had been about eleven hours. They'd gotten up early to romp around their big new house.

Sandy prepared a nice meal while Nicky set the new dining room table. Cooking was easy. Sandy just selected three boxes of ready-meals and popped them into the preparer. She was too tired to make something fancy. Out came a disposable plate with piles of food on it. There were steaming vegetables and succulent protein slices. There was hot bread with melting butter on it, and sweet, juicy fruit. She poured milk from the milk tank. She set the dial to thin for her, and thick for Nicky and Kevin. That's how they all liked their milk. She poured pure water from the house supply for Father.

Meanwhile, Nicky grumbled a little because she had to set the table by hand. Sandy had insisted on old-fashioned utensils and plates and things. They were all stored in a nice-looking hutch. But it was not robotic and would not set the table for them. Nicky did it.

And Kevin brought out the food. That's what he did.

And Father began reciting scripture. That's what Father always did.

Then, each was expected to first give the Lord thanks. Father encouraged more praying after meals, too.

They had a great lunch together. Everyone grew happy and laughed. Each told stories about the day.

After lunch, they told the door to lock. They had the hallway tiles lift them to their bedroom floors to sleep. They were all too tired for stairs. The Great Computer turned off the lighting to make it easier. And they all slept.

However, one would get up long before the others and have some great fun.

Chapter 12 – First Afternoon

Midway through the afternoon sleep-time, Kevin woke up. It was still very exciting living in this strange new place. To have a bedroom so big that you couldn't even throw as far as the far wall! He dressed quickly, and snuck downstairs, being careful not to make any noise. He went to the front door, but suddenly felt very hungry. He went to the kitchen. While rustling up something to eat, he made a noise. He turned sharply. He'd left the kitchen door open! He closed it, ate, and then went to the front door. In a whisper, he told the Great Computer to unlock and open it. It did. Out into the afternoon he went, the door closing automatically behind him.

There was no one in sight. All was quiet and still. The clouds raced overhead, as usual. Kevin went around behind their house, to the Port Gate in the big south wall. He fingered the controls to the door, but just couldn't figure out how to open it. He looked around. There to his left, between the wall and the enormous utility yard, was the shelter with all the sand buggies. Kevin raced over.

There they were. He counted. Twenty of them. Many different shapes and sizes. They were dull white but covered with dust and dirt. Some dents and scrapes, too.

He crawled into one. He pretended he was driving all over the planet in search of the very best treasures. He was so busy, that he didn't notice someone come up beside him.

"What are you doing, Kevin??" Nicky stood with her hands on her hips.

Kevin jumped up from the seat in great surprise. He bumped his head into the ceiling of the little buggy, and then bounced back down to the seat. He slipped off and landed on the floor, his arms and legs waving up in the air as he struggled to get back up.

But he grinned after getting back in the seat and said, "It would be so much fun to drive this! But how do the controls work, Nicky?" He hadn't been able to get the buggy to do anything. However, he knew Nicky could figure it out.

"Kevin, you can't ride these. They belong to the miners. We'd get in trouble."

"No, Nicky, they're all asleep! The other kids say they never go anywhere in the afternoon. No one will be up until sunset. Come on! If we just drive it around back here behind the utility yard, no one can even see. Is Sandy up?"

Nicky glanced in the direction of their house, a cube so big they could see it in the distance above the utility yard wall. "No, I was quiet. I couldn't sleep."

"It's kind of fun here, isn't it?" He grinned as big as he could.

"Yeah, kind of." She looked up at the wall around the utility yard. "I'd love to get in there and look around. That's where the Great Computer is." She looked at her wrist computer.

Kevin did, too. "Hey, Nicky! Ask the G.C. how to start the buggy!" All the kids called the Great Computer 'G.C.' or sometimes 'the big G.C.'

Nicky looked around. There was no one in sight. It *would* be fun to ride a buggy. She put her hand on the little door of the buggy. It was cold metal. They could just ride it a little around here, and then put it back. Just a short, little ride...

She began speaking with the G.C. through her wrist computer. At first, it didn't want to tell her how. Only the miners were supposed to control the buggies. But Nicky knew how computer minds worked. You just had to fool them into changing priorities. The miners had told the Great Computer what permissions to give the new missionary family. She began quickly discussing these.

Kevin grew bored, got out of the buggy and began exploring the others. Each had the exact same control panel on the dash board. Poking out of the dash board was a bright metal stick with a black knob. It moved up, down, and sideways. The stick also could twist and slide in and out. Kevin was sure this made the buggy move in all sorts of directions. He was dying to work it for real!

Kevin skipped back over to Nicky, who was now sitting in the sand buggy. She was looking back and forth at its dash board and her little wrist computer. He reached over the door and began tugging at her sleeve impatiently.

Nicky shrugged him off. She had talked the Great Computer into telling her how to start up the buggy. She was now studying her little wrist computer's screen closely.

Kevin leaned in and looked at it, too. He began tapping his fingers on the door. Well, it was obvious to him. He reached over to the shiny dash board, to where little shapes had been drawn. He quickly poked and touched the same shapes displayed on Nicky's wrist computer.

The dash board lit up with different colors and the sand buggy began to whir! Nicky yelped and almost jumped out of her seat. "Kevin!"

Kevin clapped his hands together and squealed with excitement. He turned, ran over, and scrambled into another buggy. He touched its dash board just the same way, and this buggy turned on, too!

Kevin grabbed the control stick by its knob, and tilted it upwards, because he felt that would make it go forward. Well, it did. His buggy jerked forward so hard that Kevin's head swung backward, and he felt himself squished back against the seat. Kevin's buggy began rolling forward. There was another buggy just in front of him! Kevin gasped; he was racing right toward it. He heard Nicky shout. But then his buggy suddenly stopped all by itself. He felt the stick snap out of his hand, and back to its center position. The buggy stopped so fast that Kevin flew off the seat, bounced off the dashboard, and fell to the floor. He jumped up, looked over at Nicky, and yelled: "Wow!"

Before she could do anything, he jumped back on the seat, grabbed the stick and yanked it down. The buggy jolted and moved backwards so suddenly that Kevin was again tossed off the seat to the floor. When he let go of the stick, it again snapped back to its center position. The buggy jerked to a stop making Kevin roll over on the floor, piling into the bottom of the seat.

He jumped back on the seat and looked around. Sure enough, there was a seat belt! He put it on. This time he moved the stick slowly, and sideways. The buggy rolled sideways! Its big, fat round tires could roll in any direction. Kevin now twisted the knob of the control stick to the right and then to the left. The buggy rotated to the right and to the left! Kevin was breathing hard and felt his heart banging in his chest. This was more fun than anything he'd ever done! He moved the stick forward and twisted a little. His buggy moved out and turned. Kevin steered it around the other buggies and out from under the covered area. It was like computer games he'd played, but for real!

Now beside the utility wall, there was plenty of open space in front of him. He slammed the stick all the way up, and his buggy shot forward, squishing him back against the seat. He heard the motor whirring, and then the wheels getting louder as he moved faster. The wind was blowing his hair. That felt great!

He flew past the corner of the utility yard. And there was his big cube house! But in the wink of an eye, he flew past that, too. The automatic mall was coming up in front of him on the right. The south wall had been on his left all along.

Kevin twisted the knob back and forth, and his buggy turned first one way then the other. Every time Kevin turned one way, his body would jerk to the side in the opposite direction. This made him laugh. He kind of didn't notice that he was rapidly heading toward the west wall. Suddenly, on the dashboard, some red words that weren't very nice began blinking. The control stick jerked backwards by itself. Kevin heard the wheels make a loud grinding sound. The buggy began shaking violently as it ground to a stop. The stick returned to the center position by itself.

Kevin sat without moving, though breathing hard. That was the most exciting thing he'd done for a long time. He heard a sound and turned.

It was Nicky riding up in another buggy. She looked angry. Uh, oh. He grabbed the stick. Nicky slowed up beside him and began her lecture. However, Kevin had his buggy turn around and roll off back the way they came.

He noticed the door in the Port Gate in the middle of south wall and turned his buggy toward it. He curved around and drove his buggy straight up to the door. But the door was too narrow for the buggy. Kevin unbuckled the seat belt. He stood up and leaned forward to look closely at the door's control panel. How could he ever figure out how to unlock it?

He heard a beep from the dash board. Looking down, he saw that his small hand was touching some of the symbols, which began blinking. He then heard a beep over at the door's control panel. Looking up, he saw the symbols there blinking in the same pattern. There was a loud clicking sound; like something important was about to happen. And it did! The great Port Gate itself slid slowly open to the side. Kevin jumped up and down in excitement and slammed the control stick upwards. His buggy jerked forward, sending poor Kevin, who was still standing, tumbling over backwards. He went right over the seat, dumped into the back storage box. His buggy whizzed through the gate and out of Town.

Nicky's buggy rolled through the gate and she began to chase him. Neither saw it but the gate closed automatically behind them.

At full speed, across the rough land, the buggy was bumpy. Kevin was having a hard time getting to his hands and knees in the storage box. He looked back. The wall around Town was rapidly getting smaller as it got farther away. Up ahead were the hills of dirt surrounding the landing field. He finally pulled himself over the seat and began trying to grab the control stick. His hand kept swinging around from all the bouncing the buggy was doing. He accidentally slapped the stick sideways. The buggy lurched to the left and began sliding sideways to the left, though still going forward. This lurch made Kevin fall over to the right. He half fell over the side of the buggy. He grabbed desperately at the door as his legs dangled outside. They fell to the ground and began dragging. He heard Nicky calling to him from behind.

At an angle, the buggy now rolled up the first ring of hills around the landing field. It tilted over sharply to the left. Fortunately, this put the buggy under him a little. Kevin scrambled and got one leg back in. Then there was a sudden bump, which bounced the rest of him back in. Finally, he was able to reach for the control stick. As he did, he moaned: "Oh, buggy, stop!"

And before he could even touch the stick, it returned to its center position. The buggy came to a stop. All was quiet. Kevin found himself praying, "Thanks! Thanks! Thanks!" to God.

There was a grinding noise. He rose from the floor of the buggy.

It was Nicky. Her buggy came to a stop at the bottom of the hill. Kevin scrambled out of his buggy, ran down, and hugged her.

"Kevin, are you crazy?!" She put her hands on her hips and scolded him.

They both looked back toward Town. It was now far in the distance. Even farther away behind it there was that scary-looking dark line at the northern horizon. This was the start of the great storms to the north, where no one could safely go.

They felt very alone. It was such a bleak, alien landscape. The clouds were flying across the dull yellow sky, as ever. Patches of the dull colored moss were here are there across the land. They were brown, dark green, a weird dark blue, and other colors. This went as far away as the eye could see to the east and west. The hills around the landing field, rising behind them, blocked their view to the south. The breeze never changed.

Kevin began wondering what was on the other side of the hills around the landing field. He had a strong urge to explore there. He was about to suggest this to Nicky when suddenly a small crack appeared in the ground almost at their feet. Smelly air shot out and up with a loud "foof" sound. They both cried in fright and began running. They bumped right into each other, staggered back, then fled toward their buggies. Meanwhile, the air from the ground sent a spout of dust high into the sky.

Nicky jumped into her buggy and rolled off while Kevin scrambled up the hill toward his. Soon his buggy was following. They raced back toward Town. Kevin discovered he could give his buggy voice commands: "Buggy, turn a little to the left! A little to the right! Steer straight!"

They reached Port Gate and discovered to their great dismay that it had closed. And there were no controls on the outside of it. They had no idea how to get back in! Suddenly, on both sides of them, two more dust spouts erupted loudly from sudden cracks in the ground, blowing upwards. Nicky and Kevin looked at each other in fear. How would they get out of this?

Chapter 13 – Life in Town

The lights automatically turned on in Sandy's room, and she awoke. What time was it? Was it time to get Nicky and Kevin up for school?

She looked at the clock displayed on the wall. Nicky had learned and told Sandy that the Great Computer could display a clock on the wall. Or any kind of picture. Just by asking.

The clock was special for the planet *Caesar* because the day was about forty-four Earth hours long. It had four periods of time — like a pie with four pieces. There was a line straight down from top to bottom. At the top was marked 'Noon,' at the bottom 'Midnight.' There was a line straight across from right to left. At the right of the line was marked 'Evening,' and at the left: 'Morning'. There were little marks for all the hours along the outer edge of the clock. There were eleven hours in each of the four periods — forty-four hours in all. An hour on *Caesar* was a little longer than an hour on Earth.

'Work time' was the piece of the pie in the upper left — the time from morning until noon. The next piece — from noon until evening — was 'day sleep-time.' Or just 'day-sleep,' as the town kids called it. There were two sleep periods because the day was so long. 'Night sleep-time' was the period — in the lower left — from midnight until morning, sometimes called just 'night sleep.' And the period in the lower right — from evening until midnight — was 'party-time.'

The hand of Sandy's clock — it had just one — now pointed straight to the right, evening; the beginning of party-time.

Through her open door, and the open skylight of the house, she faintly heard the voices of men from far away yelling and laughing. She got up, dressed, and trudged out to find something to eat. Father was still asleep. His snoring filled the house, large as it was.

In the dining room, Sandy found Nicky and Kevin sitting at the table ravenously eating. They looked a mess. "Go take showers before you go out," she commanded as she headed into the kitchen.

Nicky and Kevin stopped eating and looked at each other. Neither was anxious to leave the house just now. The dust spouts outside the Port Gate had frightened them and both had fled away in their buggies. When the spouts had stopped, they had slowly rolled back to Port Gate to figure out how to get back in. They didn't want to use any of the other gates for fear someone would see them come through. Nicky had spoken with the Great Computer, but they were not authorized to open the Gates. Then, Kevin remembered what he had touched on the dashboard to open the Port Gate before. He did it again and it worked! In they slowly rolled, looking all around. It had still been day sleep-time, and no one was around, except a robot or two. They put the buggies back and skittered home. And they were hungry!

It was the family's second party-time on *Caesar*. Sandy woke up Father, he ate, then set off with his Bible to again try and lead the miners to Christ. Sandy's heart burst with pride and compassion for her father and his mission. She, in turn, set out to meet the local kids again, and teach them about Jesus.

Nicky and Kevin only wanted to stay at home. However, they discovered something very special about their house.

They went up to the fifth floor. They used the tiles that lifted them from floor to floor like an elevator. They were staring in fascination up at the night sky with the glowing clouds moving along. All of a sudden, Kevin had an idea. He commanded the tiles to form a stairway from the fifth-floor hallway, up through the opening in the ceiling, to the roof. And they did! Kevin, fearless, raced right up the stairs to the roof. Nicky followed. Halfway up, she made the mistake of looking over the side of the stairway. Far below was the garden; almost one hundred feet down. This gave her an awful feeling. She jerked her head back and closed her eyes. She quickly told the Great Computer to have tiles form a wall on both sides of the stairway. She opened her eyes, placed her hand safely on the newly formed low wall, and went on up to the roof.

There was nothing on the roof. It was just the flat white building material like the rest of their house. Kevin and Nicky spent most of party-time looking down, watching the activity around town. Nicky instructed the Great Computer to make a warning sound whenever Kevin got within two steps of the edge of the house. At the lights of the meeting hall, at the center of Town, they could see and hear the miners loudly carrying on. They watched the kids of Town playing nighttime games here and there.

And so, began their new life on *Caesar*. Each morning the miners would all fly off in search of treasure. Father would offer to go along and help. But the miners were suspicious and always refused. Father would also study the Bible for long hours and go for walks. Sometimes he'd try to talk with the miners' wives. They would not say a word to him, but turn and hurry away, as if in fear.

MISSIONARY KIDS ON TREASURE WORLD – PART 1

Sandy, Nicky, and Kevin went to the school. The computers there taught them, and the miners' wives supervised. The computers taught reading, writing, and arithmetic. They taught science, plants, animals, and other things. The town kids loved learning about animals. There were none on *Caesar*. Nothing was taught about the other worlds of the Galaxy. Nicky was sad about this. At her schools before, she had loved learning about all the other exciting worlds.

They had recess often. They played with the other children and got to know them. They often saw the robots going about their duties. The robots would always wave and display smiles. They seemed to be programmed to like kids.

Some of the miners' wives were friendly to the three new kids. Sandy tried to tell everyone she met about Jesus. Nicky was amazed at how little the other children knew about the rest of the Galaxy, about science, about Christianity, about...well almost everything! Kevin tried to talk other boys into going outside the town wall. They were all deathly afraid to, because of the ghosts.

After school, the three missionary kids had chores to do at home. None of the villas had laundry machines. Everyone had to march over to the common laundry building near Laundry Gate in the middle of Town's west wall. Sandy enjoyed this, and Nicky hated it. So, Nicky and Kevin would go to the farm store for fresh food.

At noon, the miners would return, and the whole town quieted down for day sleep-time. The robots would all go off to work on any equipment causing the miners trouble — only if it was quiet work.

In the evening, it was always party-time. Each evening, they could faintly, and sometimes loudly, hear the miners carrying on. None of the miners ever came over to visit the missionary family. Not even Mr. Flan, the first miner they ever met. They saw him once flying home at noontime. He did not even wave.

Party-time was playtime for the town kids. They seemed rather subdued and overly cautious to the three missionary kids. The boy Fanson, who was fourteen, always seemed to appear when Sandy was outside. Shyly, he asked question after question about other worlds. Sandy had been on many. She tried to talk to him about his soul, his heart, spiritual things, and, of course, about Jesus. He liked some of the stories about Jesus. Then he'd grow bored, begin looking around, brush the hair from his eyes, and start scratching.

He was the oldest. The rest of the children were younger than Sandy; most were ten or younger. Fanson's father, named Fan of course, had been the first to purchase a wife from the awful space traders who sold people. The other miners were too busy spending all their time looking for treasure, back in the early days. Fan seemed to enjoy himself more. He seemed to work harder at finding treasure. Some began to say that he had more than anyone. No one knew for sure. Like all the others, Mr. Fan kept his treasure chamber locked up. But it wasn't locked up as well as he thought.

The other miners wanted to be like Fan. So, they bought wives, too. They called them 'wives' but there was no wedding, really. Beginning with Fan, each time a miner bought a wife, at the next meeting of all the miners at the meeting hall, he would tell all the others: "She's mine, and all of you stay away from her or I'll..." He would threaten something awful.

The miners wondered if the missionary man would buy a wife the next time a space trader came.

Chapter 14 – The Trash Fling

It was the day of Kevin's first trash fling.

All the kids went streaming out of the school at one of the recesses. As usual, most of the boys went to play 'miner.' They had built a pretend little Town with little bits of stuff they had found around the town dump, up in Town's northwest corner. There was a little meeting hall at the center, storage domes forming a ring around it, and villas forming a bigger ring, and a fake wall around everything. The boys had pretend fly-cars and they'd all pretend to fly off in search of treasure — like their fathers.

Kevin found this dull and pointless. He sat on a bench made of spare house stuff and blew bubbles with his bubble-bottle. Some of the other boys flew their little pretend fly-cars over and landed all around Kevin. He pretended not to notice.

One of the boys pointed to Kevin, grinned at the other boys, and cried: "Look, men, it's the Great Bubble Ghost!"

"What should we do?!" cried another boy.

"He's after our treasure. Get him!" cried still another.

All their fly-cars took off and began circling around Kevin. Kevin grinned and decided to play along. He jumped up on the bench and blew bubbles at all the other boys running around him. They laughed and attacked all the bubbles with their fly-cars.

Then they demanded that Kevin let them play with his bubble-bottle. However, he'd done this once before, and one of the boys had run off with it. He hadn't gotten it back for hours — not until Sandy complained to the wife running the school that day. Kevin was lucky she had been one of the friendly wives.

Kevin refused. An older boy stood forward with hands on his hips. He stuck his hand out and said loudly, "Let me play with that!" It was Flydeckerson. Kevin didn't like him because he was always envious of Kevin's bubble-bottle — something he didn't have and couldn't get; even at the automatic mall.

"You tell him, Fly!" That was Flydeckerson's best friend: Fotinkson. Kevin didn't like either of them. The other boys began urging Flydeckerson on, too. Kevin looked at them all suspiciously. He'd learned some of their names. Floteson, Flanson, the Folorson twins, and one named Fatspaceson or something like that. None had ever been friendly to him.

Kevin wasn't a fighter. He was more of a runner. Sensing trouble, he turned and jumped down from the bench, but there were other boys there waiting for him. They grabbed for the bubble-bottle. Kevin quickly stashed it in one of his big, baggy pockets, and tried to run off. But they knocked him to the ground, and all began trying to pile on top of him. Kevin squirmed and struggled with all his might to get away, but there were too many. He kept hearing Flydeckerson yelling: "Get the bubble thing! Get the bubble thing!" Occasionally, he would see Flydeckerson's mean, leering face; the meanest face Kevin had ever seen.

All of a sudden, Kevin heard Flydeckerson scream in pain. Someone shouted: "Get up and get off him!"

It was Sandy! And she had Flydeckerson by the ear. She was older and much taller. Flydeckerson had to stand up tall on his tiptoes to keep his ear from being pulled off. Sandy began lecturing him sternly about how wrong it was to bully smaller boys, and how much it displeased God. At the sight of Kevin's angry older sister, the other boys all fled.

Flydeckerson begged her to let go. She demanded that he first say he was sorry to Kevin. He finally did, and she let go his ear. He grabbed his sore ear with both hands. He looked angrily at Kevin and let out a big belch at him, just as one of the miners would. Then he stalked off after the other boys.

Kevin grinned up at Sandy. But then Sandy began lecturing poor Kevin at not doing a good job getting along with the other kids. Kevin hung his head and felt awful. He was hoping Sandy would have given him a nice hug. Now nobody liked him. He kicked at the ground and waited for her to finish.

Finally, she did, and led him back to school.

Once inside, it was safer because the teacher was there watching closely. It was Mrs. Flan. Kevin thought she was all right.

Flydeckerson plugged in to a learning station next to Kevin's. After a while, when Mrs. Flan wasn't looking, he looked sideways at Kevin and hissed, "You know what today is, new kid?"

Kevin said, "No. Christmas?"

Flydeckerson wrinkled his nose and made a face. He'd never heard of Christmas, anyway. He turned to the boy on the other side of him. It was Fotinkson. He'd followed Flydeckerson, like he always did. "Hey, Fot, new kid doesn't know what today is."

Fotinkson said, "Dumb new kid!" And he belched to show his disgust.

"It's Trash Day, new kid. And you better not go, because if you do...We're going to *get* you!"

"Yeah, Fly, let's fling him up with the trash!" said Fotinkson. The two boys began snickering.

Kevin moved off to another learning station. What a dumb planet! He wished he were up on a spaceship somewhere.

It was indeed Trash Day. The trash fling would be just after Day Sleep, the beginning of party-time. It was still light enough to see the trash cube flung high in the sky.

The missionary family was sharing a meal in the dining room. The girls had decorated it. There were some Picture-Windows® showing pleasing scenes from around the Galaxy. And they'd hung curtains and put candles on small tiles that they'd ordered to stick out from the wall. Father was always pleased whenever his daughters did things like this. It secretly reminded him of his lost wife, but he never talked to them about this.

Nicky and Sandy were both quite excited about the trash fling — something actually happening in the dull town. Father was quiet about it; he didn't seem to exactly approve. Kevin wasn't looking forward to it at all. He was surprised that his sisters were excited. Sometimes, he couldn't figure them out.

Father had them all pray before dinner, which was delicious. Even to Kevin. Sandy was an extraordinary cook — especially for her young age. But she would always say something that she thought was wrong with her cooking. Nicky would laugh and tell her it was great. Father would pat his stomach, then have them all pray after the meal, too. Those prayers always seemed the most fun for Kevin. No one hurried him through them. He didn't like to pray out loud in front of other people. And he was slow at it.

They all trooped off to the trash fling. Father insisted that they all participate with the rest of their neighbors.

They found the rest of the townspeople gathered over by the trasher, a small building where everyone brought their trash. It was next to the eastern wall and just south of Trash Gate, which was in the middle of the wall. This was the gate Kevin had tinkered with when the missionary family first arrived. To the north of the trasher building was the large, sewage treatment building that made loud flushing sounds all the time. Mr. Flan's villa was the one nearby, to the west.

Again, Nicky noticed the small patches or stains of different colors here and there along the eastern wall. No one would tell her about them. The town kids would just shrug and turn away when asked. Sandy and Kevin didn't care anymore.

The trash catapult was next to the trasher, just to its south. The catapult looked something like a giant spoon holding a big, dark cube. The cube was all the compressed trash of Town. This trash could not be recycled and used for anything else.

Most of the miners were standing around, fists on hips, waiting for the fling. Their wives and children were behind them. Kevin saw Flydeckerson. The gang of boys that usually was with him was with him tonight. Flydeckerson saw Kevin looking at him and made threatening signs with his fists. Kevin looked away and gulped. For some reason, he thought about King David in the Bible.

The miners wore baggy shirts with weird patterns of black and white, dark baggy trousers, and black boots. The miners never wore anything with colors because they thought this was 'girly.' Some wore caps with wide bills — the ones they wore when mining. They kept the sun out of their eyes when looking through the nuclear moss for treasure.

The miners were talking about the miner who would be firing the canon at the trash. It was Fockleberry's turn. The missionary family kept hearing the miners belch loudly. Father explained they were fond of expressing emotion in this way.

Some of the miners brought forth little nuggets of treasure. They began betting with each other on whether or not old Fockleberry could hit the trash cube tonight. Apparently, the cube of trash was unusually dark. This made it challenging. The belching grew louder as the miners grew excited over their wagering.

Fockleberry came marching up with the remote control for the canon. The canon at the four corners of Town wall were swiveling as he practiced with the controls. He was grinning from ear to ear. He was dressed like the others. He was nearly all bald, and his forehead was so low that Nicky wondered how he had enough brains to think. She giggled this thought to Sandy. Sandy jabbered her with an elbow and hissed: "Don't make fun of neighbors!"

Another miner, at the trash cube catapult, yelled, "Are you ready??" He was holding a control lever. The miner at the catapult — Fumk was his name — let out a loud, sharp belch. Fockleberry seemed to answer with another loud belch.

Sandy commented with disgust: "Ee-ew-uh…"

Nicky looked up at her quickly, and said, "Don't judge your neighbors!"

Both girls glared at each other but chose not to begin a word battle; not with Father nearby, anyway.

But it was time for the fling!

Kevin was looking around for the other boys and wasn't paying attention. The sound of the great catapult spoon snapping upward made him jump. He turned to see the great cube of trash soar upwards with a loud 'whoosh.'

The miners, their wives, and children all began either cheering or jeering Fockleberry as he worked the remote control to aim the canon at the trash cube. This was actually practice in case outlaws like space pirates ever attacked Town.

When the remote control showed the canon aiming where he thought the cube would be — and the miners were good at calculating such things — Fockleberry fired all canon.

Four bright streaks of different colors flashed up from the photonic canon. One streak was bright blue, one yellow, one white, and one a shimmering, twisting rainbow of all three colors.

All four beams hit the trash cube, now a tiny dot high above and a little to the east. It exploded into a bright expanding ball of yellow flame, then white and black smoke. Brightly glowing pieces drifted downward towards the east, and the smoke was blown to the west by the prevailing wind way up where the explosion had been. Nicky noticed that this was the opposite direction of the breeze near the ground that always blew to the east. This troubled her, so she decided to ask the Great Computer about this later.

The rest of the crowd, even the missionary family — except Nicky — made sounds of amazement and approval: "Ahhhh...ohhhh!" Some of the burning debris, that was high up and slowly falling, burst into more bright fireballs. This was great entertainment for the townspeople.

Some of the miners began arguing over the amounts of their wagers. When three or four grew angry, one very large miner — named Filchasen — put his big arms out and around the others and began pushing them toward the meeting hall. He was half-bald, and his remaining straight black hair hung like a curtain down almost to his shoulders. He said loudly: "Ha! Ha! Ha! Just drop it and let Filchasen buy you all a drink. You'll find what you lost tonight out in the moss tomorrow!"

Something had been lost? Kevin went to investigate as the crowd began to break up. The miners headed toward their meeting hall for party-time. The wives were returning to the villas. The town's children went in all directions to play or prowl the night.

Kevin went over where the miners had been arguing. There on the ground was a small object. He picked it up and turned it over and over in his hand. It was the most remarkable stone he had ever seen. It was a motley pink of many different shades with shiny golden thin squiggly lines all over it. As he turned it over and over, the tiny gold lines changed and moved. He was astonished. It was wonderful!

But it was not his, he realized. He glanced in the direction of Father walking back toward home with his great arms around Sandy and Nicky. How could he ever be as big as his father? But Father always said he would.

Kevin turned and looked toward the backs of the retreating miners, who were already starting to laugh and slap each other on the back — getting in the mood of party-time. Without thinking much, Kevin called out: "Someone dropped this treasure!"

Every single miner's head snapped around to stare at Kevin. He gulped. The sun was setting behind them, far in the west. This made the miners look like big, hulking demons. None of them ever stood very straight. Almost all were bald or balding. And what hair they had left was always hanging unkempt because they didn't wash so much. Kevin could tell this whenever he was downwind. The other kids always joked about anything as smelly as 'being east of a miner'.

Over to the side, Kevin was aware that Flydeckerson and his gang were moving closer. However, so were the miners. Kevin could not take his eyes off the miners' eyes. They were dark and surrounded by craggy wrinkles and were blinking. Most of the miners had beards of different lengths and cuts. The ones without, certainly had not shaved lately. Kevin saw teeth here and there as some grinned darkly.

Suddenly, four stepped forward all talking and trying to be heard over the others: "That's mine!" "Back off, Fearbiter, it's mine!" "Fumk, you're a dead man if you touch it! I dropped it!" "Give it to Fatspace! Give it to Fatspace!" "You always do this to me, Folor!"

As they rose in front of him, Kevin gasped and took a step backward. He couldn't breathe. And it wasn't because he was downwind from them.

The largest miner of all, Filchasen, loomed up behind the four. They were bending forward sticking their big hands toward Kevin. Kevin kept backing up. Filchasen peered at Kevin and blinked. "It's the God-man's kid!" His voice was so loud, low, and booming that Kevin felt it in his bones. "What you got there, kid?"

Kevin slowly lifted his hand. His whole arm was trembling. He opened his hand to reveal the shimmering pink stone.

"*Gold fissionate!*" some of them gasped.

"That's mine — I dropped it!" cried Fumk. "No, mine!" growled Folor. "Give me that treasure!" demanded Fearbiter. "Fatspace! Fatspace! Fatspace treasure!" howled Fatspace. Fatspace began throwing a tantrum. (Early at the beginning of Town, before space traders began arriving regularly, Fatspace had experimented with distilling his own liquor. His experiments had not worked out.)

Filchasen swore using some very ugly words. "Let the kid have it. You know the rules. No fighting over anything or you lose your turn at everything."

"Fatspace fling trash! Fatspace fling trash!"

Filchasen clapped Fatspace on the shoulder. "That's right, Fatty. Your turn next."

Folor growled: "Ehhh, we'll find more on the ground tomorrow, boys."

And from behind, one of the miners called, "Remember rule number one..." And several of them all said it at the same time: "Treasure's not yours until it's in your chamber!"

"Yeah, keep it, kid," said Fumk. "Go buy your dad a wife!"

They all laughed loudly as they turned and trudged toward meeting hall.

Kevin turned to go home but was surprised to find Flydeckerson and his friends standing in the way. They looked mean.

Kevin yelled: "*Sandy!*"

Flydeckerson stuck out his hand. "Give it to us!"

Fearbiterson next to him said: "And the bubble thing, too!"

Kevin's grip on the stone tightened and he took a step back.

Sandy stormed up behind the younger boys. In her most nailing voice, she began condemning them for their mean behavior. The boys jerked up and swung around in surprise. Her scolding was hot and fiery. They wilted in spite of themselves, and all slunk away. Kevin wondered how she had such power over kids.

And then, again she started lecturing Kevin over doing such a poor job at friendships. He ground his teeth with frustration as he followed her back home. His fists were so tight that the stone hurt. But it began to grow too hot, so he stuck it in a pocket.

Nicky had waited and joined them walking back. Father seldom noticed what went on among children. He was always thinking about how to save this world. They all went home to bed.

It was not the last time Flydeckerson would be after Kevin.

Chapter 15 – Downward

It was night sleep-time. Kevin heard knocking at the front door. No one else got up to open it. So, he got up and went quietly downstairs.

At the door, he found Fotinkson, Floteson, Flanson, the Folorson twins, and another named something like 'Fatspaceson'. Flydeckerson was there, too.

Kevin wanted to be their friend. So, he took them to the kitchen and got them something to eat. Then, he had an idea to get on their good side. He quietly told the tiles to make stairs. He led the gang up level after level, past Sandy's floor, past his floor, and past Nicky's floor. They finally arrived at Father's floor. He was snoring loudly. Strangely, the other boys didn't notice it at all. Then, Kevin told the tiles to make stairs up to the roof. Up they all went.

It was eerie up there in the night with the glowing clouds of different color flying overhead. It made the other boys all sorts of weird colors. All of Town was dark and quiet. They all turned and looked over the edge of the big opening in the middle of the roof. The garden was so far down below that it made the hair stand up on the back of their necks.

Up until then, the boys had been friendly to Kevin. He thought they were going to be his friends. However, Flydeckerson now frowned and stuck out his hand, which was very dirty. He demanded Kevin give him the bubble-bottle and the magic pink stone.

Kevin was flabbergasted. His feelings were hurt, and he felt crushed and betrayed. The stairs back down were a few steps away and he suddenly felt he better get out of here. He took a step, but the other boys were in his way. Flydeckerson told the other boys to "Get him!" And poor Kevin felt himself grabbed all around. "Toss him over the edge!" ordered Flydeckerson.

Kevin yelled and tried to struggle free, but they held him with surprising strength. And they dragged him to the edge until he could look over and see the garden far below and all the tiny night lights down there. Kevin began shouting for Father and Sandy to come help. Flydeckerson and the other boys only laughed cruelly.

"Give us what we want or over you go, new kid."

"Over you go, new kid! Over you go, new kid!" the other boys chanted again and again.

"Give us what we want, and we won't throw you in," said Flydeckerson.

Kevin stuck his hands in his pockets and gave them what they wanted. Of course, he wanted to live more than he wanted his favorite toy or even treasure.

Flydeckerson grinned at him, turned, and hurled Kevin's beloved bubble-bottle high into the air. It disappeared over the side of the villa, surely to be smashed to bits on the ground far below. Kevin moaned in horror.

Then Flydeckerson took the pink stone with the shiny moving gold lines and bit it between his gnarly yellow teeth. He actually chewed it up and swallowed it. He grinned at Kevin, and there were the tiny gold lines squiggling all over his teeth!

Flydeckerson giggled and said: "Throw him in!"

Kevin cried: "You said you wouldn't!"

Flydeckerson laughed and laughed.

"Over he goes! Over he goes!" yelled the other boys as they dragged Kevin to the edge.

Kevin screamed for Father, Sandy, and Nicky. Again and again, as loud as he could, but there was no response. How miserable and alone Kevin felt!

And then, with a final push, over the edge they threw him.

He began to fall. There went Father's floor past him. Then Nicky's and Sandy's. He was falling so fast. Then another floor, and another, and another. And the floors whizzing past him got stranger and stranger...

Kevin's eyes snapped open and he sucked in air as hard as he could until he couldn't suck in any more. He looked around. It was dark and quiet. It was his bedroom! He looked over the edge of his big bed. Floor!

He looked around again, blinking, he couldn't believe his eyes. He was okay! "It was a dream!" he whispered. He gnashed his teeth and growled a little. "I hate bad dreams," he said to himself. He wished more than anything that his mother was still alive. He felt an ache in his chest like there was a hole in it. Now there was no one to love him and hold him anymore. Even Sandy was mad at him because of the other boys. And Nicky was nice but always thinking about other stuff. And he loved his father with all his might, but Father was always working on saving everyone.

Kevin got up and dressed. He pulled out his beloved bubble-bottle. It was perfect! He blew a few bubbles. They stuck together and danced merrily around when they got near the little holes at the top of the wall that blew in air.

In another pocket was the pink treasure stone. How the golden lines glowed even in the dark!

Kevin decided right then and there that he was going to find enough treasure out there to buy his own spaceship and fly away to wherever he wanted to go!

He quietly went downstairs, stuffed some food in his pockets, and left home.

It was dark outside, and no one was around. The glowing clouds moved silently overhead. Kevin shivered. He wasn't cold. He said to himself, "It was just a dream."

He told the door to lock itself, and then went around the villa and over to Port Gate. But he still didn't know how to unlock the little door in it. He looked to the left. There was the building with the sand buggies.

In a few minutes, the biggest sand buggy rolled up to Port Gate. Kevin stood up from the pilot chair and pressed the symbols on the dash board like he'd done the first time. He was really good at remembering stuff like that. He never even had to do homework much like other kids. He always remembered everything. This made Nicky very happy.

As Port Gate began to slide open, Kevin turned and waved at his villa. He said sadly: "Good-bye, Nicky. Good-bye, Sandy. Good-bye, Father."

He would send them all a postcard from the big, exciting jungle world that he planned to buy with all the treasure he was about to go get.

His buggy rolled out and into the night.

Back in the villa, Sandy finally awoke. Something had been bothering her night time dreams. She listened carefully but heard nothing. Had she heard something? She thought maybe she had. Or it was a dream. Suspicious, she put on her nice pseudo-satin night gown from the automatic mall. It was so smooth from being made of modern material. She couldn't even feel it against her skin, though it kept her quite warm. And if it wasn't tied, it wouldn't stay on. Sandy secretly loved clothes. However, she refused to talk about it like other girls her age always, always did. But now, on this new world, there were no other girls her age. She went downstairs.

At least there was her sister, Nicky. At the thought, Sandy looked over the edge of the balcony up at Nicky's floor. All quiet. She felt warm inside about her sister. How she loved her more than anyone! Except Father. She loved him completely, too. Her family was everything to her. And she loved Jesus with all her heart, her strength, her mind, and her soul. She was so proud to do so.

She sighed. Even her little brother she loved. Why was he always in trouble?! She quietly made the exasperated throat sound. Little brothers! Then she grinned. He was so funny, really, blowing bubbles all the time. And he was quite a clever little boy. And he had always been gentle and never broken anything that she could remember. If only mother were here, all would be perfect. Dear mother, whom Sandy would see again in heaven.

The front door was locked. There was no sign of anything out of place. She went back to bed and fell quickly asleep.

Where to go? Kevin drove the buggy around aimlessly. Town was in the distance. All he could see was the wall and the little lights at the four corners where the canon were. There was plenty of light to see by from the glowing clouds of color above and the shimmering gray behind them. Kevin looked around the buggy. Colors weren't as easy to see in the dimness, though. He pulled out the pink stone. It looked light gray now. He asked it: "Tell me where there's more!" He hoped it was a magic stone that would talk. But it said nothing. He held it up to his ear. Still, nothing. Hmphf! Stupid rock...

Where was all the treasure? Where did the miners go to get it? Kevin began to think. Well, he really didn't want to go where they went, because it would all be picked over; there'd be no treasure left for him. He noticed the hills, in the middle of which was the landing field for trading ships and the shuttle that had brought his family. It seemed so long ago now.

Kevin gasped. Behind those hills! He was suddenly quite sure that none of the miners had ever mined behind those hills. The hills were, after all, in the way. Nothing behind could be seen from Town.

Kevin set off at full speed. The buggy went around the ring of hills, and Town disappeared behind them. Kevin had expected to see treasure lying all over the place. However, it was just like everywhere else. Except there in the distance! There was something sticking up. He raced the buggy over to look.

It was a bunch of craggy, dark rocks sticking out of the ground, as big as him; some bigger. He drove the buggy around it. They formed a sort of crown shape with nothing in the center; just flat ground. Kevin got out to explore. The hair on the back of his neck went up. But he ignored this.

The craggy rocks turned out to be very spindly and complex; sort of like foam that had been stretched and then frozen. He touched them. Extremely rough!

There were actually lots more than he thought, and they weren't as thick together as they had looked. He walked and squeezed between them until he was at the center, which was a completely open area. He walked across it and counted a dozen steps. This open area had a slight bulge upward to it. He could feel it as he walked over it. He thought of the domed treasure storage chambers of the miners. Maybe he was standing on the greatest chamber of treasure in this entire world! And only he knew of it! But how to get in.

Kevin jumped up and down, slamming his heels against the ground. Nothing. He thought maybe he'd hear a hollow sound. Perhaps he hadn't jumped hard enough. He jumped again, and again. He began running all around the cleared area jumping up and down as hard as he could.

Suddenly, there was a loud "phoof!" sound from behind. He turned then jumped back in fright. A dust spout was exploding from a big black crack in the ground. The crack was getting bigger with an awful grinding noise. The spout was loudly shooting high up. It was the biggest one he'd ever seen. The swirling dust and dirt was glowing gray in the night light. Kevin's eyes grew wide. He thought he could almost see a face in the swirling, twirling clouds of dust. Like a dust ghost in the night!

Kevin turned and ran for the other side of the clearing, toward the buggy.

He was about over to the other edge when there was an explosion of dirt and dust right in front of him. Another dust spout blasted out of the ground, up and up, until high overhead. It was bigger and louder than the first. Kevin cried out, turned, and ran another way. However, another spout erupted near the edge where he was going, with another scary looking black crack in the ground. Then he heard another blast of dirt and another, from one direction and then from another. And the ground seemed to be shaking a little. Then dust was blasting all around until he couldn't even see anymore. Where was the buggy?? How could he get out of this? He blinked and rubbed his eyes. The sound and wind of all the dust spouts roaring all around was terrifying. He wished he was dreaming again so he could just wake up from it. He jumped up and down to wake himself up.

Suddenly, there was a crunching sound beneath him, and the ground was gone beneath his feet. He fell in. His arms hit the edge of the ground on both sides of him. He stuck them straight out to keep from falling into the hole that was opening below him. Air and dust and dirt were blowing up from it, stinging his eyes. He cried out in fright, "God, help! Help me!" He scrambled to grab something, but there was nothing to grab. He slipped and slipped. He screamed, "Oh, God!" And down he went into darkness and noise.

Chapter 16 – Foofs!

Nicky awoke. What had been that noise? She sat up in bed. She asked the Great Computer. It had been Sandy going down to the door and back to her bedroom. Nicky could plainly hear Father snoring — her bedroom was on the floor just beneath his.

She got up, went to the balcony overlooking the central opening of the house, and looked down at the beautiful nighttime garden far, far below. The tiny nighttime lights were slowly changing colors. What a wonderful new life they had! So much to learn about. An entire world! She had a feeling there were many adventures in store for them all.

She had a sudden urge to check on Kevin — as if something wasn't quite right. But, no. Sandy had just been up. If anything was wrong, Sandy would have taken care of it. Sandy was just like mother had been — sort of. Not exactly. Nicky sighed. They all missed Mother so much, yet not one ever talked about it. Kevin especially. Nicky vowed to herself to be nicer to him and reach out to him more. He needed his big sisters. Especially, with all the aggressive little boys he played with.

She thought about checking in on him. He was just in the bedroom on the floor below hers. But he'd wake up for sure, and then wouldn't go back to sleep, and then somehow wake up Sandy. And she'd get mad at them all.

Nicky crawled back in bed. It was so perfectly snug! The modern bedding from the automatic mall actually snuggled up softly against her all by itself. And the clever pillow knew how to keep her head at just the most comfortable position, no matter how she was lying. Nicky was a tosser and turner. But she now felt so comfortable and secure that she easily fell back into soft sleep...

Kevin had finally come to a stop. He was now in complete blackness. He hadn't moved since he had landed. At first, he had fallen and fallen; the wind ripping past him. He couldn't breathe. It had been so terrifying that he couldn't even think. Then, as he fell, he banged up against something; like the side of a mountain — he couldn't see because all was darkness. And he slid along this; and then tumbling, until he stuck his arms and legs straight out. And then he slid and slid. Then he hit something and tumbled out into nothingness. Then *bash!* against the mountain again. Sliding, tumbling, rolling, sliding. More bumps. More flying through the air. He crashed through pockets of some kind of soft dirt that sprayed up all around.

It was all getting hard to remember. He had finally stopped. Then, he had stood shakily to his feet in the pitch-blackness. He'd taken a step, and then tumbled off into nothingness again. And then more sliding and tumbling.

Now he had come to a stop and didn't dare move. He had stopped breathing hard. His body felt beat up. But nothing felt too painful. He was a thin boy and had always bounced rather well.

He blinked his eyes. It was so dark, that it didn't matter. He only saw blackness. It looked the same, eyes closed or opened. He dug in a pocket. He was thankful his trousers hadn't come off!

Thankful? Kevin began whispering everything he was now thankful for to God. Then he asked the Lord to save him. He waited.

Nothing happened. Father always said that the biggest part of the answer to any prayer was time.

Kevin found something in his pocket and slipped it onto his finger. He pulled out his hand and turned on the flashlight built into his ring. He adjusted the beam to be wide. He flashed it around. He was lying in a pile of yellow, sparkly sandy dirt. A slope of the same colored stuff stretched upwards behind him; not too steeply. There was more of the stuff in every direction. Above him, was blackness. He turned up the light to full. Blackness. He made the light a thin beam. There was dust in the air, so he could see the thin white line of the beam as he swung it above him and all around. It went on almost forever and dwindled off to nothing in the distance. Where *was* he?

He made the light wide again. He slowly and carefully got to his feet; looking all around in case there was anywhere to fall again.

"Hello?" he said aloud. His voice was flat and muffled. There was no echo.

It was warmer down here. But there was no sound. He turned off the light. Blackness came in from all around. Frightened, he quickly turned the light back on. The hair on the back of his neck went up. He looked up. Nothing. Blackness. Where was home?

He sank to his knees, bent over, and began to cry. What had he done?? He was now lost and gone. He felt big tears rolling down his face. More than he could ever remember crying. Even when Mother had gone...

Oh, now why had he thought of her now?! He shook himself, trying to get angry to make the feelings go away. But he was now overcome with such grief, that he just curled up on his side into a ball and cried and cried.

A long while later, he woke up. He had fallen asleep. The ring was still lighting up the area. He didn't think that it ever wore out. Good!

He remembered something important. He began to pray to the Lord to save him. Father said that if you really needed something, you prayed again and again. So, he prayed and prayed.

He prayed aloud, and he prayed in his head. He stood up, and then hopped up and down in anger. He threw his arms up in the air and prayed loudly. He fell to the ground, stricken with grief, squirmed around in the sand and prayed more. Finally, he was all prayed out.

He felt hungry. He reached into other pockets and found the food that he'd stashed. Was it ever mashed up! But it sure was delicious...

What was that?! He thought he saw some kind of light in the distance. It was dim. He turned off his ring light. The blackness enfolded him like someone throwing over a blanket. There in the distance, not his level but higher up. Faint, lights. Or, faint round glowing things? He shouted, "Hello!" They seemed to move and then disappeared.

He hated the darkness and turned his light back on. Weird.

He remembered the other boys talking about the ghosts. Ghosts!

He started feeling fear rise up. What did Father always say about ghosts? He couldn't remember anything. Sandy loved to tell that story of King Saul going to the Witch of Endor and raising the ghost of the prophet Samuel. There *were* ghosts!

Then he remembered Father reading once from a really old Bible. The words were all different and hard to understand, and it was holy ghost this and holy ghost that.

Holy ghosts? Kevin tried to convince himself that maybe some ghosts were good, holy.

His hand brushed against a big bulge in his pocket. The bubble-bottle! He pulled it out. It wasn't broken by the fall! It really *was* made for kids.

To make himself feel better, he began to blow bubbles. They looked great in the bright light from his ring. He would blow for a while, then open the little slide panel on the bottom of the bottle with the controls that made the bubbles burst by remote control. Nicky once explained that it had something to do with sound that he couldn't hear. He made lots of bubbles then made them all burst. There was nothing else to do, except maybe explore some.

He turned to figure out which way to walk. There were the lights again! But much closer. They were pale round things for sure! And colored. A pale pink one. A pale yellow. And a pale green. It was hard to tell how big they were far away in the dark.

Kevin's bubbles were settling around him. In annoyance, he pressed the button at the bottom of the bubble-bottle and they all burst. There was a sudden humming sound from the direction of the round, colored things. They began moving rapidly. Two bounced together, and then all three disappeared behind something.

Kevin waited a long time. He began to feel alone again. With the round things, at least there was something else here. He had an idea and blew some more bubbles; bigger ones.

The yellow glowing thing appeared slowly; just like a half-moon. It was peeking out from behind something. Kevin shined his flashlight ring that way. It was almost too far to see. He thought he saw maybe a rocky wall.

Kevin set the bubble-bottle controls and blew big colored bubbles, making sure some were yellow, pink, and green.

This made the three glowing things totally come out. And they came closer. And closer. Kevin's eyes widened. They were round like balls and were floating. Floating like bubbles! Each one had two flat, black spots, side by side in front, near the top. They were perfectly round. Eyes, for sure! And each pair was looking straight at Kevin.

They slowly floated closer. They were smaller than he was, but bigger than any ball he'd ever played with. The pink one actually had a round green area at the top. The edge of the green area was saw-toothed. The yellow one had a thick, dark blue band around its middle. The edge of this was wavy. And the green one had large white round areas on its sides where both its arms sank in; the edges of these areas were fuzzy. Kevin thought these extra highlights made them all look rather fancy.

Arms! Each had thin, black things sticking a little way out on each side; just where arms would be. At the end, they forked into two little black fingers. Underneath each creature, Kevin saw a pair of thin, short black dangling legs, each ending in a thick black pod.

And that was it. No mouth. No nose. No ears. Nothing else.

Remembering how a person had to be around animals, Kevin moved slowly. He reached out a hand, and one of his bubbles landed on it. They were set for 'tough' and wouldn't pop until he made the bottle send out the pop command. As soon as the bubble landed on his hand, he began hearing a soft, buzzing from first one of the ball things, and then the other two. And he began smelling the most pleasant fragrance; like flowers. He found himself smiling.

"Who are you?" he asked.

The three creatures all began moving erratically, even bumping into each other. They moved farther away, and finally settled down. Kevin couldn't see what made them move. They had no wings or fins or fans.

Kevin put the bubble-bottle in his pocket, held up his other hand, and let another big bubble come to rest on it. With his hand turned upside down, his light ring lit up the ground brightly. This lit him up and the bubbles he was holding.

The three glowing balls came up to him again. And now Kevin heard the most amazing sound. Each was making a kind of puffing, hissing sound. And they were taking turns. One went: "Foof, foof." Another went: "Fooof. Fff, fff, fff. Foof!"

The green one went, "Foof, foof...fffoof!"

The other two both turned to look at the green one. Both began foofing at it loudly.

Kevin grinned. This was great! He himself said, "FFOOFF!"

The three stopped foofing, and all slowly turned toward him. Each one's big black pair of eyes slid close together, as if they were peering

116

closely at him. Could they ever stare! The eyes were like two black holes, each about the size of Kevin's fist.

The pink one's eyes now squashed flatter and wider, and Kevin heard "Fooofff" from it.

Kevin quietly said, "Yes, foof. Foof to you... you foof!"

The eyes got round and big again; and then suddenly narrowed to straight up and down slits. Then they went round and slid apart until almost to the thing's sides, above its arms, which now were waving up and down.

Kevin began to smell something awful, like burning rubber.

The other two, the green and yellow ones, turned toward the pink and began foofing loudly. And then, extraordinarily, the colors of the two began changing! Slowly but steadily. Kevin saw every color of the rainbow. However, only ever two colors at a time.

They began a long conversation of foofing back and forth. The pink one remained pink, and finally seemed to calm down. The bad small went away.

Kevin held out his two, big bubbles, and this got their attention. Their colors returned to the original yellow and green and pink, and the highlights. They stopped foofing and floated closer to examine the bubbles. They were very close now. However, Kevin felt no danger. They were just big floating balloons, after all. Looking closely, he saw that they were actually fuzzy. The fuzz was thick and fine, covering them completely.

The green one slowly reached forward a thin, black arm. It got longer and longer, coming out of its side until longer than Kevin's arm.

It touched the bubble, twiddled it a few times with its fingers, and then said, "Foof!"

It pulled its arm back inside itself, turned to the other two, and a long foofing talk began again among them.

Kevin thought to himself: *I've discovered Foofs!*

As he watched, their talk became wilder. The arms of the green and yellow one stuck all the way out and began swinging in circles. The foofing got louder, and the three were all foofing at once. Kevin looked closer to see where the foofing sound came from. They were so fuzzy. Here and there, the fuzz was shaking really fast. This made the foof sound!

Suddenly, the green one began to grow bigger and bigger. Kevin took a step back. Then, with a great hissing sound from beneath it, it zoomed straight up. Kevin felt a slight breeze blow against him. The foof came to a stop far overhead.

The eyes of the other two had slid to their tops to watch.

Kevin slowly moved the bubbles that he'd been holding to the ground. The pink and green foofs turned their big black eyes to watch him. When Kevin stood back up, his light ring was aimed at the foofs and lit them up brightly. The black disks of their eyes shrank down to just black dots.

They were bright and shiny in the light. Kevin thought they were beautiful creatures and wanted to reach out and touch them. But he thought it might scare them. He looked up. The green one was still far overhead just floating.

The yellow now stretched up and down somewhat, until egg-shaped. Then it returned to a ball, and said, "Foof. Fffooff. Fffff."

Kevin said, "I don't understand you."

The two foofs moved back suddenly, in response. Kevin felt a slight blast of air against his face. They floated towards him again. And then, he heard his very own voice come from both foofs at the same time, saying: "I don't understand you."

He pointed to himself. "I am Kevin." He pointed to them. "What are you?"

There was some quick foofing between them. The yellow one said, "Kevin you. Kevin are you?" It was speaking in his, Kevin's voice!

Kevin said, "Yes, I am Kevin." He pointed to it. "You are a foof. Fooofff!"

The two now looked at each other. Each said "Fooofff!" exactly as Kevin had. They began making a high-pitched buzzing sound, like a dentist's drill. Their eyes had flattened to black lines straight across. One said, still in Kevin's voice, "I don't understand you."

The other said, "I am foof. You are Kevin." They both started the high buzzing again.

The yellow one turned to Kevin and said: "I understand Kevin. Kevin understand foof?"

"Yes," answered Kevin. He wanted to teach them more words. He pointed to his light ring. "Light ring. This is a light ring." They both repeated this. He pointed to different parts of his body and told them the word for each. They repeated every time. He taught them the word for the bubbles that were still on the ground. He picked up a handful of dirt and named that. Then he pulled out his bubble-bottle. They were fascinated. He blew some bubbles with it. The foofs went crazy! Their eyes slid to opposite sides of their heads, they suddenly smelled bad and began moving around rapidly, bumping into each other a few times.

The commotion attracted the green one, who floated back down. There was some intense foofing between all three. Kevin now heard them saying his words from time to time. The pink and yellow calmed down and came to a stop. The green one shrank smaller and slowly approached Kevin's large bubbles still on the ground. The green one's eyes slid to the back, glanced at the pink and yellow one, and then slid over and up to look up at Kevin. "Bubbles are foof? Bubbles not foof?"

The green one was now using words like the other two! Kevin thought they must have taught him. He had been too high up to hear them.

Kevin answered, "Not foof. Bubbles are bubbles."

The yellow one said loudly, "Bubbles are bubbles!" and began the high-pitched buzzing sound. The pink one moved suddenly and bounced the yellow one. The high buzzing stopped.

Kevin tried talking with them as much as he could. It was hard without much of anything to point to. He used his hands a lot. And tried to act some things out. Then he squatted down and began drawing on the sandy ground. He told them the words for what he drew. The foofs loved this, and began drawing in the sand with their thin, dangling legs. But they were slow at it, and only could draw thin lines.

Working together, the three foofs made a drawing. Kevin examined it. There was a straight line. Then several large circles touching one side of it. Then a little farther away were several smaller circles, about half the size of the big ones. Kevin turned his head this way and that, and suddenly figured out that the straight line was the ground, and the circles were foofs. Whenever one of the foofs would draw two arms sticking out of one of the circles, the other foofs would do the high buzzing sound. They also drew legs connecting the larger circles to the long straight line. Here and there among the large circles were small dots that the foofs had drawn by just poking a fingertip. Sometimes the dots were grouped together touching. Kevin thought of his bubbles.

The pink one shrank a lot smaller and floated down very close to the drawing. A bulge appeared in its body near one of the little drawings of a foof. The bulge grew until it touched and covered the circle. The foof waited a moment, then floated upwards, inflating again. The bulge smoothed out.

The drawing of the foof was now colored the same pink color as the foof itself. All three foofs made the high buzz. Kevin decided they must be highly amused.

Kevin scratched letters in the sand with his finger. He wrote his name and got them to understand that this was the same thing as him saying it. One of them scratched a perfect copy of his name in the sand. He wrote and taught them other words. The foofs were delighted with this, it seemed. The fragrance of flowers was strong. And their eyes squished down to flat lines.

Kevin found that the foofs always remembered everything he taught them. This was quite satisfying. He loved remembering things exactly, too.

Kevin wanted to ask them if they believed in God and knew about Jesus. But he couldn't figure out what words to use. He couldn't figure out how to teach them anything but simple words. He drew a cross in the sand. But the foofs didn't know what it meant. He tried to draw a man hanging on the cross. Kevin wasn't much of an artist, and the foofs didn't understand. If only Nicky were here! She could explain anything. And she was a great at drawing. *And if Sandy were here,* he thought, *she could teach them about Jesus!*

Kevin tried to tell them that he was from high above. And that he wanted to go back up. They didn't seem to understand. Kevin suddenly felt very tired. He sat down and began to cry. In their own language, the foofs conversed with each other, from time to time, pointing toward Kevin. A few times, they said his name and other words. He didn't care.

He felt quite hopeless. He had no more food and now he was sure that he would just die here. He'd never see his family again. Big tears rolled down Kevin's face.

At the sight of the tears, the foofs showed signs of being distressed. Then, the pink and yellow ones shrank a little smaller and floated down until they were on both sides of Kevin. They slowly floated over until they were touching both sides of him. They were actually warm and soft. He faintly heard humming and buzzing sounds inside them. These were strange but comforting.

The green one suddenly foofed something, then inflated bigger and bigger, then shot straight upwards. Up and up until Kevin couldn't see it anymore. He wondered where it was going.

He lay down over on his side, curled up, and closed his eyes. He felt the foofs squishing down over him like warm blankets.

Where was he? How could he get out? While praying to the Lord to save him, he fell asleep.

Chapter 17 – Special Rock

Kevin awoke at the sound of voices. They all sounded like him. "Kevin go." "Kevin stop?" "Kevin move?" "Kevin move up!"

He opened his eyes and sat up. He had no idea how long he had slept. There before him were the three foofs again. Kevin blinked. There was also a flat piece of rock, about the size of a desk top — and it was floating a foot or two off the ground! The green foof floated just above the rock. It was holding the floating rock steady with one arm. This arm reached down and disappeared into a small hole near the edge of the top.

Kevin slowly stood up blinking at the floating slab of rock. It was thick and flat. He aimed his ring light at it. The top was polished and shiny. It was mottled green with little black dots all over. The edges of the rock were very rough, as if broken away from something. Kevin looked underneath the rock. Nothing there.

The foofs began the high buzzing at this. Kevin stood up. He knew this meant they thought he was being funny.

The green foof now reached down with its other arm. There were some pebbles here and there in shallow holes along the edge. Kevin looked closely. The pebbles were twice as long as they were wide. The foof lifted some, turned them sideways and placed them back in. Some pebbles were now set in deeper; some now shallower. Kevin looked closely at the holes and discovered they had slots across at different levels. So, by lifting and turning a pebble, it could be put back at a different height. Each pebble was a different color. They had bands around them. Some were shiny, some dull.

124

As Kevin watched, the foof manipulated a few of the pebbles. The rock then slowly moved downward and came to a rest in the dirt. With its big black eyes, the green foof looked at Kevin. It pointed to the rock with one arm and pointed straight up with the other. It said, "Kevin move up to the surface."

Kevin grinned. The foofs knew what he wanted to do! They remembered every word he ever said, and always quickly figured out the meaning. They had understood when he had pointed to the surface and told them about it. He had tried to scramble up the slope behind him – only to slide back down. And the foofs thought this had been funny.

The pink foof said, "Kevin stand on..." It floated over to the rock and pointed. "What called this?"

Kevin replied, "That's a rock! A big rock."

"Kevin stand on rock. Foof move rock to surface."

Kevin jumped on the rock. Glancing at the control pebbles in their little slots, he remembered something. Reaching in to a pocket, he took out the pink stone and showed it to the nearest foof, the green one. Its eyes became narrow slits and slid apart some. It also began shaking a little.

With a sudden loud hissing sound, the yellow foof zoomed over. It snatched the pink stone out of Kevin's hand, and then held it against its middle.

The green foof stuck both arms straight out and began waving them. It began foofing so loudly that Kevin could feel a little breeze from its shaking fuzz.

The pink foof, with arms reaching forward, floated toward the yellow one.

The yellow one backed up, inflated bigger, then zoomed upwards, and curved away. The pink one inflated and zoomed after it. They chased each other all around. Sometimes, they zoomed closely past Kevin and the green foof. The yellow one tried a few times to hide behind Kevin.

Finally, the green foof floated upward and inflated until it was bigger than even Kevin. It began making a loud, low booming sound. Kevin had to cover his ears it was so loud; like someone hammering on a gigantic bell.

The other foofs returned. The green one foofed at them for quite some time. It then stuck out an arm.

Kevin didn't see the yellow foof holding the pink stone anymore. But then the yellow one reached up, stuck its arm into its middle, and pulled out the pink stone. The green foof pointed to the pink foof. The yellow handed over the stone, and the pink one pushed it into its middle until it was gone. The green one now deflated down to the size it was before.

The pink one's eyes drifted to opposite sides of its head. Kevin smelled the fragrant, flowery smell that he thought meant a foof was happy or content. The pink foof began slowly drifting downward.

The green and yellow foofs began foofing. The pink one withdrew the stone and passed it to the green one. It pushed the stone into its middle and reacted the same way.

Eventually, it pulled out the stone, and handed it back to Kevin. Kevin looked. It was still pink but there were no more little golden lines. He looked at the foofs. They were all floating near the ground, very content it seemed. Kevin stashed the stone back in his pocket.

126

Kevin sat down on the rock and wrapped his arms around his knees, hugging himself into a ball. All three foofs looked at him. Each pair of eyes had moved close together. They looked at each other and began foofing, sometimes making the high buzzing.

The green one inflated some, floated over to the rock, reached down and grabbed hold within a small hole. It foofed at the others. The yellow one floated over and grabbed on, too. The pink one hesitated. The other two foofed at it. It still hesitated. The green and yellow foofed louder, and now slowly turned white. To Kevin's astonishment, their eyes changed from round to square.

Finally, the pink one, its eyes far apart, as if looking in all directions at once, boarded the rock.

The green foof moved a few of the control pebbles and the rock began to rise. The pink foof extended its thin black legs and planted its thick round feet to the flat surface of the rock. As the rock moved faster, the green and yellow foofs were blown over the edge and were dangling. They slowly struggled back on and planted their big round feet.

The rock moved up and up. Kevin aimed his light ring all around but could only see the steep nearby slope moving past. The green foof was looking up. Now and then, it would adjust the control pebbles. The air blowing over Kevin grew stronger.

After a few minutes, the foof brought the rock to a stop. To Kevin's surprise, a strong breeze kept blowing down on them. The three foofs had pulled in their legs and were sticking close to the floor of the rock. The green one foofed to the others, then said: "Kevin see big place big."

With that, it stuck its legs out farther, slowly waddled over to another part of the rock, and moved around some pebbles there.

Light began to glow from beneath the rock; a white light. It grew brighter and brighter. Peeking over the edge, Kevin could see the slope dropping far, far below. He was sure high up! Kevin skootched a little closer to the very center of the rock. The other foofs looked over the edge. The pink one extended its legs a little too far, and the breeze blew it right over the edge. Its legs bent over the edge like black cords. But its feet stuck firm. Its two arms shot all the way out. The point at which the arms connected to the foof's body slid around behind the foof. This let it reach back farther. Both Kevin and the yellow foof reached out to help. The two foof's grabbed hands. Their tiny pair of fingers made a strong link. Kevin felt the two fingers of the pink foof's other hand pinch tightly around his finger. They pulled but couldn't get the pink foof over. The breeze was blowing too strong. The pink foof now turned orange. Its eyes were at the sides of its body.

The green one foofed loudly. The pink foof, over the edge, shrank smaller and smaller until they were able to pull it back over. And there was that awful burnt rubber smell.

The foof composed itself — turning pink and then making its top green again.

The green foof moved more pebbles. Kevin was astounded by what happened next. His mouth fell open at what he saw. Here and there, and as far away as the eye could see, bright lights turned on. Kevin saw that they were inside a cave — actually a gigantic cavern! It was bigger than any inside place he had ever heard of. So big, that he couldn't even see all the way to the other end. The lights that far away just became a haze.

He now saw that the slope they were nearby was a towering rocky structure. It looked like someone had stretched it up from the cave floor, then up and up, until taller than a skyscraper building of a modern city. It was very sandy, and Kevin had slid down all this sand. Here and there, was a large, stretched out hole all the way through the structure.

He looked around the immense cavern. There were other tower rocks just like this one; some close, and many far away. They looked like water thrown from a pail, suddenly frozen, and stood up on its end. And with sand poured down all over. And there were lights here and there as far as he could see. On another nearby rock tower, he saw that the lights were other flat rocks, like the one he was on. The light was coming out from underneath them.

He looked down. The floor of the cavern was flat. It was the same dull yellow color as the sand of the nearby rock tower. There were a few rocks and boulders of different sizes scattered around. None of the lights shined upwards, so no roof of the cavern could be seen — just darkness.

As soon as all the lights had been turned on, all three foofs looked around in fascination. Their pairs of eyes would slide to another part of their body, stare from that point, then jerk to another point. Kevin watched in amazement. Their eyes could slide to any part of their bodies; except where their arms and feet came out.

They had all been watching for only a short while when the yellow and pink began foofing wildly at the green foof. And there was the burnt smell of rubber. And two kinds of it!

The green one foofed back and its eyes became triangle shaped. The other two foof's eyes became square shaped and they foofed louder. They were foofing the exact same sounds at the same time, over and over. The green foof's eyes became round, slid to the opposite side, and Kevin heard it give a quick "Foof!" Then it reached down and manipulated a control pebble. All the other lights faded out until the great chamber cavern had disappeared into darkness. The bright light below their rock stayed on.

The green foof slowly waddled back to the edge it was at before, being careful not to get blown away by the breeze. The foof made the rock begin rising again.

Their rock followed the slope of the great towering slope upwards. A few times, the slope went through tall holes to the other side of the rock structure. When they went through one of these, their rock brightly lit up the sand below. The reflected light lit up the entire hole.

Now and then, the rock structure had twists and spirals. They followed each of these up and up.

The rock structure began getting wider. The green foof had trouble finding where to go and went back and forth several times. Sometimes it would stop to decide. The breeze was blowing down stronger than ever now. To keep from blowing away, all three foofs had shrunk down to almost the size of a human head. The little green foof looked quite strange with its long black arms sticking out.

The holes through the rock structure were now short caves going up and up, like wide chimneys. These chimney caves were brightly lit up by the floating rock's light as they passed through. The foofs glowed pink, yellow, and green in the eerie, reflected light. The wind was now noisy and howling slightly.

Finally, they began going up one chimney cave where the wind was so strong that the rock slowed to a stop. The green foof manipulated the control pebbles, and the rock started moving upwards again. Kevin looked up and felt his heart jump. He could see night sky through the hole at the top of the chimney cave!

Sure enough. The hole got bigger as they approached, and he saw more sky. The wind howled noisily. The floating rock slowed down again from the strong wind blowing in through the hole. The rock began moving downwards. Faster and faster! The green foof tried moving the control pebbles. But the wind was now blowing the poor little foof so much that its arm flopped back and forth and couldn't get to the control pebbles.

The floating rock banged against the side of the chimney cave. Kevin fell over on his side. There was a loud scraping sound as they dragged along the rocky side of the chimney cave. Kevin heard low, booming sounds coming from the foofs. All their eyes were on the opposite sides of their bodies making them look crazy. Kevin began crying out loud for God to save them. He could hardly hear himself in the howling wind.

Their floating rock moved away from the chimney wall, and banged against the other side, even harder. So hard that Kevin was rolled over and over. He would have gone over the edge if he hadn't stuck both his arms and legs out wide to stop the rolling. He felt his foot bang against the wall of the chimney cave; felt it scrape as their floating rock sank downward.

Kevin turned and scrambled desperately across the rock toward the green foof and the control pebbles. Kevin had watched closely as it had moved the pebbles. He thought he knew which pebbles to move. Now the green foof called his name. It was trying to tell him what to do. Kevin could hardly hear because the wind was so loud. He moved pebbles the way he thought was right. They slowed their downward movement. The rock began lifting them up again!

The wind was so strong that Kevin remained flattened out on the rock. He was afraid of being blown away. He hoped the little control pebbles of the rock didn't get blown away. But they had a curious way of sticking to their slots. He felt a strange buzzing or humming through some of them.

The rock rose through the hole at the top of the chimney cave. Suddenly there was sky everywhere. It was beautiful nighttime sky of *Caesar* with all the beautiful moving colored clouds. He was back at the surface! Kevin was so happy he felt tears in his eyes. He yelled thanks to God out loud.

They were in the middle of the ring of craggy rocks. There was his sand buggy on the outside! But the sandy clearing that had been in the middle of the rocks was completely gone. It was now the top of the chimney cave they'd just come out of. And they were still rising!

But there was no big wind now. There was just the constant, sideways breeze to the east.

The green foof worked the control pebbles to bring the rock to a stop. It was having trouble because its arms were shaking. And it seemed to be having trouble with its eyes. They were just thin, straight up and down lines. And they kept sliding to both sides of its body. It needed them in front to see the control pebbles. The other foofs looked the same. And they were still making the low, booming sound. Kevin was downwind from the green foof. It was making that awful burning rubber smell again.

The rock floated down and over to the edge of the hole, coming to a stop. Kevin got to his feet and jumped off. He grabbed a craggy rock, in spite of himself. He was half-happy to be back, and half-afraid of falling back down.

He looked back at his friends the foofs. What was he now to do? He had to go home. Now tears really started pouring out of his eyes. The rock with the foofs was beginning to sink back down the hole. He heard them calling his name. He heard them saying over and over: "Kevin! Foofs! Again!"

Then they sank from view and were gone. He still saw the glow of the rock's under-light. But this faded and was gone. There was just the wind blowing down the chimney cave.

Kevin looked around in sudden fear. What if the miners found out that he'd poked a hole in the planet?! He had to get away before he got caught.

He quickly scrambled through the rocky crags to the buggy. He was so thankful it was still here. Suddenly, he was so thankful to be back on the surface. He fell to the ground, right down flat on his face, and began telling God how thankful he was — just like Father said they did in the Bible.

Chapter 18 – Back Home

Finally, Kevin got up, wiped the wetness from his eyes, and crawled into the buggy.

As he drove back toward Town, he wondered what he was going to tell everybody. Would he ever be in big trouble! He'd poked a hole in the planet and it was sucking in all the air! What if they ran out of air?! He gulped. He would need to talk to Nicky; she'd know what to do. He definitely didn't want to tell Sandy. She'd kill him!

He looked around. It was still nighttime. He must have been down there for a day or two, he thought!

Kevin rolled up to Port Gate, tapped the dash board command to open it, then rolled in slowly and quietly and put the buggy right back where he'd gotten it. Then he crept home.

Once in the house, he found the tile stairs just as he had left them. Quiet as a mouse, he crept up to his room. He was really hungry but would wait until morning to eat. He didn't want to wake Sandy.

In his room, he closed the doors. Then, he went into the bathroom. Kevin looked around at the huge chamber. He said to himself, "So many big places here!"

His clothes were a filthy mess from sliding down the sand and rocks. But there had not been a tear or ever a scratch. They'd purchased clothes on a modern world before coming to *Caesar*.

He took a shower with his clothes on to get them all clean. He didn't want his family to know where he'd been. Kevin couldn't stand the thought of Father being unhappy with him; like back on the spaceship after *that* trouble.

Out of the shower, he stood in the dryer booth until both he and his clothing were completely dry and fluffed out. He changed to nightclothes and flopped into his bed. His wonderful, soft, warm comfortable bed! He couldn't help grinning from ear to ear. Never had anything felt so good before in his entire life.

He was asleep before another thought crossed his mind.

Chapter 19 – Secret

Kevin had barely been to sleep, it seemed, when he awoke the next morning to Sandy shaking him. He had to get ready for school.

He was quiet at the breakfast table. Everyone else chatted on about their life there. Kevin wanted more than anything to go back and see the foofs again. Were there more of them? He remembered their drawings. Did they live in that empty chamber or were there other chambers to explore? Chambers full of foofs! Kevin imagined there were secret chambers all through the planet *Caesar*, even to its very center.

He looked at his family and wanted to tell them, of course. But then he thought about the big hole sucking in the air. He'd get in trouble — big trouble — for sure. He kept quiet and would not tell them yet.

It was another typical day. Father tried to make friends with the miners and go with them mining. None would have him. So, he spent the morning studying God's word, praying, and walking all around Town. Sandy, Nicky, and Kevin went off to school. Nicky vacuumed up knowledge as fast as the computers at school could show it to her. Sandy tried to teach the other children about Jesus every chance she had. They were so unresponsive! It frustrated her greatly. She tried to get Nicky to help, but evangelism was just not one of Nicky's gifts. Sandy would think of the great evangelists of the Bible. She sometimes spoke with her father about the frustration of trying to reach these stubborn people. He would tell her that sometimes to be successful you had to reach beyond reach.

Kevin dozed off several times in school that day.

Several days passed. Nicky began making friends with the other girls, and a few of the boys. The way they all played was often too rough for Nicky. She would sit someplace quiet and tell anyone who would listen about what it was like on other worlds. She was good at telling people about things and places. She became popular this way. But a few were a little jealous of her.

Some of the kids told her a little about their home lives. They were dismal and sad stories. The miners were not nice to their families at all. Some of the things Nicky heard were shocking, and she would not believe them.

Sandy wasn't there to make friends. She was there to lead people to Jesus. That's how *she* thought about it, anyway. She loved her family with all her heart, and *they* were her friends. Even Kevin.

The boy Fanson seemed to like her more and more and was always following her around. Sandy couldn't decide if she liked this or not. He didn't get in the way, though. And, for some reason, it was pleasant when he was around. Sandy supposed that he was cute. Perhaps, she would discuss this with Nicky.

Sometimes he would do something silly, probably to impress her. She would just stare at him. And then he'd begin to behave himself again.

Once, she found him playing a game called kid-toss with the other children. A bunch of the kids would stand nearby each other, and then Fanson — the biggest — would pick up a small child, take a running start, and throw the child at the other kids. The object was to see how many would fall over. Sometimes, Sandy learned, the kids got hurt. From this and other rough play, kids were now and then taken to the clinic building where robot physicians would fix up wounds and set broken bones.

Sandy was appalled at this. She patiently explained to Fanson just exactly why it wasn't right to hurt other people. This thought was something new to him. Sandy asked him what his father would think. Fanson burst out laughing, something he rarely did. As a matter of fact, this was the first time Sandy had seen him laugh about anything.

The other young boys continued to taunt and tease Kevin. This made him furious. He longed to toss Flydeckerson down the hole he'd made out beyond the landing field. They knew that Sandy would always come to Kevin's rescue, so they always waited until she was far away to really let poor Kevin have it. Kevin longed to escape his dismal life in Town and go visit the foofs. He'd been thinking about this more and more.

One evening, Kevin stood before the door in Trash Gate. There had just been an exciting trash fling. It had been Mr. Fatspace's turn. He couldn't talk well but he sure could shoot the trash out of the sky. And he was known for being the best at finding treasure. The other miners would have been jealous, but Mr. Fatspace wasted a lot of time finding his way back to Town because he often got lost.

The boys had bothered him yet again, and he was tempted to sneak out right now and go try to find the foofs. He didn't have a buggy, though. He wasn't sure if he wanted to go out beyond Town without one. The sun had just set, and it was getting dark. If there were foofs underground, who knew what creatures might be out there lurking in the dark. Ghosts? The miners never went outside Town after dark. And there was no one Kevin had ever heard of who was tougher than those miners. Kevin learned that their miner fathers threw some of the boys around the house. This was on days when they didn't find as much treasure as they wanted. One boy had laughed and said his father was so strong, that he could throw him up against the ceiling. The boy had rubbed a large bruise, which was still sore. Another boy boasted how his father — in a great rage after his treasure had fallen out of his fly-truck — had thrown the boy out of the house through a window. These stories left Kevin rather stunned and speechless. His own father only ever touched him to hug him. Sometimes — and this Kevin loved — his father would be in a rare, silly mood, and he'd tousle Kevin's hair.

As Kevin stared at Trash Gate, someone poked him painfully in the ribs from behind. He whirled around. It was Flydeckerson and his gang. Kevin looked quickly around. Sandy and his family were nowhere in sight. And everyone else who'd watched the trash fling had gone off. He was alone with this bunch.

They began taunting him. And, as it was dark, and no one was around, they seemed meaner than usual. Kevin had a sudden idea. He grinned and told them that he was just about to go out, and would they like to go with him? Flydeckerson gave a sinister laugh and said he knew that no one could open the door. Kevin said that *he* could and that the other boys were really just too scared to go out, because they were "town boys." That word had just popped into Kevin's head.

The other boys looked at each other repeating it: "Town boys?"

"Yes," said Kevin, arching his eyebrows high. "We space travelers aren't as afraid as you ground-livers." He made up that neat word, too.

They began to act confused. Kevin taunted them more. It was great that the table had turned.

Then Flydeckerson smacked his fist into his hand. He demanded that Kevin open the door if he could. Flydeckerson didn't think that he could. He was ready to pound Kevin for making fun of them.

Kevin turned quickly and tapped the code into the door lock. He was suddenly worried. He'd only done this at the Port Gate. Would the same code work here at Trash Gate? He gulped. If it didn't, then he was in big trouble. He looked back at the others and grinned a little sheepishly. Flydeckerson growled, "Well, come on, new kid. Open it!"

Kevin finished. And waited. He held his breath.

There was a click and a whir, and the door opened.

The other boys stared. They hadn't seen outside for a long time. It was rare that their fathers took them out mining. And the miners never took their families on fly-car trips beyond the walls of Town.

Kevin walked out, turned, and began making fun of them for being so cowardly. He began dancing around as if he owned the place.

The other boys looked around to make sure no one saw them, and then slowly crept outside.

Kevin waited by the door while the other boys walked around in awe at being out on their own for the first time. Kevin was trying hard not to grin or burst out snickering. He quietly stepped back through the door. He slammed it tightly closed behind him. The locking click was the most satisfying sound that he'd ever heard.

He wished that he could hear them better. The great wall rising high up muffled their frightened yelling. Their pounding could barely be heard through the thick door. Kevin snuck away at a trot.

He decided to take a stroll to the automatic mall to buy a little snack. To celebrate. Father had given him some allowance money that day.

Kevin grinned from ear to ear all the way there.

Chapter 20 – Dinner

"What's taking so long?" Sandy shouted from the kitchen.

Nicky had been setting the table for dinner. She appeared in the kitchen doorway. "I had another...vision."

Sandy looked up from her work with the machines that were preparing and cooking their dinner. Her expression was blank. She didn't always know what this would mean.

Nicky beckoned, "Come see."

Even the large dining room table they'd purchased at the automatic mall seemed small compared to the giant dining hall of their home. Like the other rooms in the house, it was so big that it felt like being in a church!

Nicky had lavishly laid out the table in an amazing new way. Nicky had used all the place settings. Every single one. Father had purchased many, in case of many guests. However, not one of the townspeople had ever accepted their invitation and come to dinner.

Sandy had insisted on gold and bone as the colors for the settings — to match their new world. Nicky had every single plate on the table connected together with all the golden utensils. Everything everywhere connected with the same pattern.

Nicky smiled in satisfaction at Sandy. "This shows how everyone on this world will be connected together in the love of God."

Sandy stared speechless at how Nicky had so beautifully and amazingly arrayed the great table.

Father arrived. They told him about the table. He nodded in immediate acceptance, as if a vision was an ordinary, everyday thing.

Everyone wondered where Kevin was. Nicky thought of asking Father to let Kevin wear a wrist computer. But she knew Father frowned on such things. She herself wasn't wearing hers to dinner. Father believed devices like that distracted and separated people from God. Nevertheless, Nicky loved hers because it helped her understand God's creation. She always wore long sleeved shirts, so Father wouldn't see it.

They enjoyed dinner together every night. The girls loved it. It was the time when Father was happiest, laughed out loud, and gave them his full attention. This was when everyone was encouraged to tell their stories of the day, as well.

Often Kevin was late for dinner. His family assumed that he was out with the other boys. Actually, he would be late because he took the long way home, to stay away from Flydeckerson and his gang.

They prayed and began dinner without him. Father was patient because Kevin was still only six. Sandy thought to herself that Mother would never have put up with it.

The food cart rolled to whoever asked for it. In the kitchen store of the automatic mall, Father had glanced at it, and thought it was an old-fashioned, wheels-only moving cart. But Sandy had ordered a fully automated one. Father didn't like too much automation. But he didn't make her take it back. He always said that it wasn't his policy to tread on his daughters' free-will — too much. Sandy smiled and told the cart to bring her the gravy. As it moved toward her, it turned so that the gravy bowl would be nearest. It kept itself at the exact height of the table. It came up against the edge. Then it slid the gravy bowl onto the table next to Sandy's plate. Sandy thanked the unit and patted its control panel. Father chuckled out loud and Nicky grinned.

They heard the front door slam. Kevin happily yelled, "I'M HOME!"

This was unusual, and they all snickered.

Kevin stomped into the dining room, grinning from ear to ear. They hadn't seen him so happy in a while.

Father pointed the way to the bathroom and wiggled his finger. This meant: "Go wash up first, Kevin!"

Kevin ran off and ran back shortly. He took his place. He was still grinning.

Sandy assumed he was pleased with some mischief. She asked suspiciously, "What's so funny?"

Kevin paused while he prepared the story. "Flydeckerson and those guys got in big trouble for being outside the wall!"

Sandy looked at him sharply. "What did *you* have to do with it?"

Kevin's eyes grew big. "Nothing! *Me?* How would I know how to go outside?" He glanced at Nicky. She looked away and said nothing.

After a sweet treat at the mall, Kevin had felt guilty for trapping the boys outside. He raced back to Trash Gate to let them back in, fearing what might happen to them. A ghost could get them. Or they might fall through a dust spout hole down into a foof cave. He almost laughed out loud at the thought of this. But as he came around the corner of the sewage processing building, he jumped back in alarm. Then, he peeked around the corner.

There was Flydeckerson's father holding Flydeckerson by the hair. Right off the ground! Flydeckerson was struggling wildly, holding on to his father's arm to keep from losing his hair.

There were some other miners there, too. The other boys were just coming in through the open door in Trash Gate. Mr. Flydecker was loud, and Kevin could hear him, as far away as he was.

"How'd you get out this gate?!" He shook him.

Flydeckerson howled in pain. He cried out, "It wasn't me! It was the new kid — the God-man's boy! He let us out!"

"Yeah!" cried the other boys.

Mr. Flydecker swung his great arm and whacked the other boys. Some fell over. Their fathers grinned and nodded approval. Kevin, from where he was hiding, blinked and his mouth fell open in shock.

Mr. Flydecker roared, "You're lying to me, boy! Them new folks don't know nothing. Now, how'd you get out there??"

Flydeckerson loudly began to cry and wail. Mr. Flydecker growled in frustration. He gave him a final shake before throwing him to the side and stalking off. Over his shoulder he loudly growled, "The code needs changing, Flart."

One of the other miners, the one named Mr. Flart, went to do something at the door. The rest turned and stumped away. One was coming in Kevin's direction!

Kevin pulled around the corner of the building and had raced home to dinner.

Now, at the dinner table, Nicky was looking directly at him, staring. She knew he knew how to get outside.

Kevin glanced at Father, lowered his head and mumbled: "All right. I let them outside."

But Father laughed and asked how Kevin could possibly know how to get through the locked wall.

Kevin was about to answer when he noticed Nicky, across the table from him, now *really* staring at him. Her mouth was a tight line.

He blinked a few times. "Uh, I figured it out."

Nicky cleared her throat and leaned forward.

Sandy leaned forward suspiciously. "Well, Kevin??"

Kevin blurted out, "I figured it out by…uhhh…pushing the buttons of the sand buggies! Then I went for a ride and went through Port Gate. And a few nights ago, I fell down a big hole and was underground all night. I met foofs!"

There was wide-eyed silence at the table. Father didn't laugh out loud, but his tight-lipped grin meant he was highly amused.

Sandy saw this, then looked at Kevin. She made that throat sound "hghghgh" and went back to eating. She began ignoring him.

Nicky grinned. "Foofs, Kevin?"

"Yeah, there are little floating people underground. Down in big chambers."

Sandy's fork was halfway to her mouth. She stopped, raised her eyebrows unbelievably high, and asked, "You've figured out how to get in to the miner's locked chambers, too? Hghgh!" She went back to eating.

"No!" cried Kevin. He began telling them all about his adventure.

Father listened to the story with patient amusement. Nicky eventually burst out giggling so much that Sandy shushed her.

Kevin said, "I'll show you!" He felt around in his great pockets. He was wearing the same coverall that he had the night of the fall. He wore it a lot to keep Sandy from harping on him about laundry. Kevin made a habit of wearing *his* clothes in the shower and then drying with them on, as he'd done before. No one else did this, just Kevin.

"Remember the treasure stone I found?" They had all seen it and were amazed. He had just told them that the foofs had eaten all the gold off of it. Now, he would show it to them to prove it.

"Look!" He held forth the shiny, pink stone.

And there were bright, tiny little gold lines all over it, again.

Kevin stared at it in confusion. He had looked at it closely down with the foofs. They had eaten off every gold line.

Sandy and Nicky giggled.

Kevin jumped to his feet. "I'll show you that I was outside!" He was furious now. He didn't even care if anyone found out he'd made the hole that was sucking up the air. Actually, after a few days had passed, since he was still breathing, he wasn't so much worried about the hole anymore.

"Come on! I'll go open Port Gate for you! Maybe there's a spaceship there at the landing field waiting for us!"

Kevin marched for the door. Father shrugged good-naturedly and suggested they follow. Nicky and Sandy fell about each other laughing and followed.

At Port Gate, Kevin tapped the code to open into the control panel next to the door. Nothing happened. He tried again. And again. It would not open.

Nicky let out a loud sigh of relief.

Father and Sandy looked at her in puzzlement.

Nicky grinned at them. "Uh, it's a good thing they change the codes around here."

Sandy made the throat sound and marched for home. Father thanked Kevin for telling such a fun story. He followed Sandy home.

Nicky turned to Kevin. "You must have had a dream."

"Nooo!" he howled. "I'll drive you out to the hole!"

He raced toward the sand buggies. Nicky went after to stop him. She was still afraid of getting the blame. She didn't want him getting in any trouble with the sand buggies.

But the sand buggies wouldn't start.

And Kevin couldn't get Nicky to talk to the Great Computer because she wasn't wearing her wrist computer.

They went home to find that Sandy had cleared the dining room table and already prepared it with evening games. The family had begun playing games together each evening after dinner. There was singing, too, and plenty of other things to do. Father didn't want the children going outside at party-time anymore.

Kevin was sullen. He began to doubt if he had really been underground or seen the foofs at all. Had it all been a dream? Like the dream of the bad kids throwing him off the roof? The only way to find out would be to go back out to the crown of rocks. He would check if the foofs were still there at the bottom of the hole.

This time, he would bring a ladder.

Chapter 21 – Sunday

It was the day everyone in Town was going to hear Sandy.

There were no days of the week on their new world *Caesar*. The miners didn't do anything regularly, like once a week or once a month or even once a year. They just always searched for treasure every day. So, they didn't need days or months. And they didn't like years. Years made them think about getting older.

The next day was the missionary family's seventh day on *Caesar*. Father decided that it would be Sunday. They had to have a day of rest every seven days. Plus, they had to have a day of worship. So, Father led them in worship. They held it in their giant entry room, big enough to feel like church. They left the front door of their villa open, in case anyone else wanted to join. Father let all three children do plenty. Each got to read from the Bible. They sang many songs. Nicky had had the Great Computer display scripture and songs on the wall in huge words. This made it easier for Kevin. He still needed a little help with some of the bigger Bible words. He was great at singing, though. They all had beautiful voices. Father had them practice regularly.

Kevin was happy that he didn't have to go to school. After worship, he stood in his room playing an exciting video game displayed all over one of the giant walls. He was yelling with excitement as he jumped around, slapping the brightly moving images on the wall to make things happen.

Nicky wanted to go to school, and asked Father if she could anyway. He said no because she needed a day to rest her brain.

150

Sandy asked if Father was going to preach, since it was Sunday. He said no, there was no one to preach to. The miners were all gone in the morning and asleep all afternoon. It wouldn't be proper to invite their wives over without them. They certainly wouldn't be happy about it.

He had brought a news show player to *Caesar* and was going to spend time catching up on the events in Christendom throughout the Galaxy. He had filled the player with fresh news just before they had left aboard the spaceship. He would also, of course, go for his daily stroll.

Sandy thought to herself: *Someone has to preach.* And she decided that that someone would be her. She marched off to find Nicky, to ask her how to get up to the roof.

Nicky showed Sandy how to tell the tiles to make the stairway to the roof. Nicky still thought it was scary looking over the edge at the garden so frighteningly far below. Nicky and Kevin enjoyed going up to the roof during party-time to watch the wild goings on around town. The robots had made their house so big! Nicky could never get the town kids to come inside and play. They were always either too scared at the enormous size or jealous because it was so much bigger than theirs was.

Nicky and Sandy both stood on the balcony of the fifth floor — Father's floor, though he was on the ground floor in his office reading Christian news. They could always tell because they'd hear him now and then cry "What?!" or groan loudly or laugh.

The Great Computer built the tile stairway to the roof. Up on the roof, they found the sun just up in the east. It was a beautiful sight. The clouds in that part of the sky were glowing gold with the sunrise. Other clouds were scudding along to the west, as usual. Far to the north, along the horizon, was the dark line of the northern storm area. Far to the south, behind the hills around the landing field, was the dark line of the southern storm area.

Kids and some of the miners' wives were out around Town. School wouldn't start for a while.

Sandy walked to the edge, looked down, and then took a cautious step or two back. The roof was a hundred feet from the ground below. She cleared her throat about to speak. She had a simple message and she knew who she was about to preach to.

However, Nicky put her hand on Sandy's arm. She said that from way up here, no one would hear her. Nicky slipped off her wrist computer from out of her sleeve and strapped it to Sandy's wrist. Then, Nicky spoke into it and instructed the Great Computer to let everyone hear Sandy's voice. Nicky knew that all over Town, anyone near a building could speak with the Great Computer and hear it. Every building had special little places in the walls. These let the Great Computer listen and speak.

Sandy saw on the wrist computer screen the words 'ON' and 'OFF.' Nicky told her these would turn her voice on all over Town or off when she was done, or if she had to sneeze or something.

Sandy turned to Nicky, smiled broadly, and said the Holy Spirit was with her. Nicky smiled, folded her hands in front of her, and bounced up and down in excitement.

Sandy turned on her voice all over Town and began her first sermon. As she spoke, her voice came out at every villa and every building. The women and children of Town heard her at the laundry and the mall. They heard her at the farm store and even the trash building and everywhere. She said: *

"I have good news for you. There is a father above all things who created you and really cares for you. He knows when you're hurting and wants to help. A long, long time ago, on the far world where everyone first came from, things were worse than anywhere ever since. Into this, a child was born. A very special child because he was sent by the father of all things. He was sent by God. His name was Jesus, and he was God's only son. God sent his only son with a special message just for us. And this special message is for you, too, people; all you people of this only town on *Caesar*.

"The message is that God likes being close to you. The creator of everything, even the planets and the stars, loves each of you and wants to be close. And he wants you to be close to him. And you know how to be close to him? Do you want to? Do you want to be close to the great, loving God of the universe who is the true source of all joy and peace? Be loving! Be loving, you people! No matter what is happening to you. No matter how other people are treating you. Be loving! Even to people who are not nice to you. Be nice anyway. You will make God happy and he will bless you by bringing joy and peace into your life.

"He really wants to do this. How could he be a god and not care for everything he's created? Why would he create so much and not care about it? He really cares about every one of you. Be loving and nice to everyone. Treat who you are with as the most important person in the world.

"God sent his only son Jesus to show us how. Jesus was very loving. He could make anyone who was sick or hurt, better. And he told

---

* Dear reader: It is more fun to stand and read Sandy's sermon out loud.

us all about God, and it was written down, and we can read about it even today.

"Jesus told us how much God loves us and cares. Jesus told us God even wants to listen to us and talk with us. You can actually talk to God anytime and he will listen. And do you want to hear him speak to you? He will, if you really want to listen. Do you want to hear God? Then begin being a loving person, and you will begin to hear him. The more loving you are, the more you'll hear him speaking to you.

"We are his children. God is the father of everyone and all things. And a father wants his children to obey. But it's easy to obey God. He asks just this: Be loving! No matter what. Like his son Jesus. When Jesus came, he was always loving. He showed us how.

"There were some very bad people back then who didn't like Jesus. They even hated him. But Jesus was still loving. He chose to be. God gives each of us the power to choose to be loving or not. And no matter what anyone else says or does to you, no one anywhere can take away your power to choose to be loving. Choose to be loving! No matter what is happening in your life.

"The evil men wanted to kill Jesus. Jesus was loving and good to everyone who came to him. And these evil men didn't like this. It made them look bad. And they were! So, they captured poor Jesus, were cruel to him, very cruel, and they killed him. It was sad. It was the saddest thing that ever happened. They placed his body in a cave.

"But Jesus was the son of God. After he had been dead for a few days, he came back to life! He went to his friends to tell them the greatest news for all time. His friends were the men and women who knew that he was the son of God. Jesus told them this good news: That because his friends believed that he was the one and only son of God, and wanted to follow only him, the God of everything had decided to let them live forever. And they were to tell everyone, everywhere the good news.

"His friends were excited by this good news. They raised their hands and told God how much they loved him. And they were loving in everything they did.

"And you, too, can live forever! Tell God that you're happy he sent Jesus, his only son. Choose at your very heart to be loving by being like Jesus. Be loving in everything you do. Tell God that you've made this choice. And God will let you live forever. Even if you die, you won't really die, just your body. God will keep you, your soul, safe. You'll be taken to a beautiful other world called Heaven where you will even get a new body.

"So, in all things God will protect your very soul. No one can destroy or take away your very soul. It belongs to God because he created it. Choose at your very soul to be loving because this is what God wants you to do. Be loving by following the example of God's only son Jesus. You will live forever. And you will one day meet Jesus and be with him in paradise. Because Jesus is God himself!"

Sandy was done. Everyone in Town had heard. She wondered what the miners would do when they found out. She also wondered if God had found her sermon pleasing.

She began to pray.

Chapter 22 – Sunday Walk

As Nicky heard Sandy's final words echoing around the town, she stared at her older sister in wonder. Nicky whispered, "You know so much about God!" But Sandy didn't seem to notice. Her face was flushed, her eyes were bright, and she was staring far away.

Nicky stepped forward to look over the edge. She expected to see a huge crowd — all of the townspeople. Instead, there was no one. Nicky wondered what everyone around Town would think. What if they told the miners? Would there be trouble?

They both heard a step from behind and turned to find Father approaching. Nicky quickly took back her wrist computer, slipping it up her sleeve.

Father embraced Sandy and told her what a good message she had preached. The two began talking about it. Nicky let out her breath. She'd been worried he might be mad.

Nicky left them and went downstairs. It was morning and she'd been in the house for such a long time — all through yesterday's day-sleep, party-time, and night-sleep. She'd been in since noon of the day before. She went outside.

She looked around, wondering what to do since it was now Sunday. She didn't have to go to school or do any work. Father said they still had to clean up any mess they made. But she didn't have to do any housekeeping. She smiled.

The door of their house was on its north side. Nicky stood in front of it looking out at Town. There were all the villas of the people. Ringed inside these, she saw the tops of the miner's precious treasure chambers. In the distance, she could just barely see the meeting hall in the center. To her right, Nicky looked at the wall around the great utility yard. She could see so many mysterious buildings and machines sticking up over it a little. She'd love to learn more, but the miners didn't want any kids in there.

To her left was the great automatic mall. She enjoyed window shopping with Sandy there. Sometimes they'd stop at the sweet shop run by robots. *Mmm,* she thought, *that sounded good.* Maybe she'd stop in later.

Beyond the mall to its right, she saw the clinic. Not too far to the right of that, she saw the school.

Kids were coming out to play. It was recess time. Nicky decided to go over and see which of the miners' wives was teaching. She could ask what the wife thought of the sermon Sandy had just preached!

On her way over, she met Fanson, the oldest boy, going the opposite way. She stopped to greet him. He brushed his blond hair from his eyes to look at her as he passed. He nodded a little and continued on his way. She knew where he was going. She snickered to herself.

At the school, Nicky peeked in. The teacher that day was Fockleberrywife. What would she have to say? She was one of the nicer ones. At least, she didn't beat the children. Flydeckerwife was one to obey and avoid, for sure. She had once almost given Kevin a beating. Sandy had stepped in front of him just in time and launched into the sternest lecture Nicky had ever heard from her — and to an adult!

Fockleberrywife was quite chubby and had lots of curly brown hair that she let down only in the classroom. She enjoyed children and enjoyed herself at the school. Nicky always wanted to give her a big hug, but the townspeople never hugged. As a matter of fact, the only time Nicky could remember them touching was when the boys fought. Or when beaten in school. She'd seen the miners give their kids a cuff now and then. Nicky knew these people needed Jesus at their hearts and soon. She wished Father would hurry up. But he would always say that there was no time to hurry.

Fockleberrywife saw Nicky and immediately began asking her about that strange message from Sandy.

Sandy, also, wanted to stretch her legs, and left the house.

And there was Fanson — as always. Before she could get flustered — she'd wanted to go for a walk by herself — he smiled a little. He had a wide mouth that dimpled at the corners when he smiled. His teeth were white and straight; not at all like most of the other children. His eyes were always two dark lines. She still didn't know what color they were. He was lean but not thin. His nose was almost pointed. Sandy suddenly decided that it was cute. And she felt herself grow a little happy just because he had shown up. This sort of bothered part of her. She smiled back at him anyway.

He said, "So...everyone heard you talking."

After a moment, Sandy raised her eyebrows and leaned forward, "And..."

"Well," he shrugged. He was wearing his rumbled, sand-colored coverall, as usual. "I was going to the sweetshop. Uh, come with me!" He stuck his hands in his pockets.

Sandy sighed, then said: "Okay."

He nodded, then turned and began walking. Sandy joined him.

At the great opening arch of the mall, the current decorations that were out and whirling around overhead greeted them both by name. It was a smart mall. They walked down the wide, center aisle looking into the bright and crazy displays in all the store windows. It was really entertaining. The oldest kids often came to the mall at party-time and walked the center aisle, back and forth, for hours just talking.

A large decoration swung down from the ceiling right in front of them. It was a clown thing with dozens of colored streamers floating and flowing all around it. It grinned and told of the latest wild drink that the Great Galactic Sweetshop was now featuring. It held up an enticing animated picture of it.

Fanson turned to Sandy. "I'll buy you one." Then he stood up straighter and said proudly: "I have money."

Her eyes narrowed a little. "How'd you get it?"

"Father now pays me to clean his equipment and his fly-car." He went on to explain that his father wanted him to learn how important money was, and that there was nothing more important.

They reached the Great Galactic Sweetshop. In the windows were amazing colorful arrangements of pretend candy-making machines. Assembly lines with every sort of candy were moving back and forth, up chained conveyers, and down spiral slides. In between, bright colored liquids shot through twisting turning tubes. Inside, there were chrome tables with bright red chairs and thick benches along the walls. No one else was there, except the attendant robots idling around.

They came to a table with two chairs on one side and the thick bright red wall bench on the other side. Sandy plopped down on the bench where she could see. She hated sitting in chairs with her back to everything. Fanson hesitated, then, awkwardly it seemed, sat down slowly on the bench beside Sandy. He was rather close; Sandy stared at him and blinked. Fanson got red in the face, then slowly got up and sat in the chair opposite her. He cleared his throat and grinned.

A robot came up and asked their order. Before Sandy could speak, Fanson ordered two of the specials: Stellar Splatter Matters.

Nicky saw by the clock on the wall that recess was almost over. She excused herself to Fockleberrywife and left the school building. She didn't want to be there when the other children returned. The teacher would make her stay.

The questions Fockleberrywife had asked about God and the other things in Sandy's sermon were so simple. Nicky was dumbfounded how a teacher would know so little about such important subjects.

She hurried over to the automatic mall. It was just a two-minute walk south of the school. Inside, the advertising decorations were all stirred up, so someone must be there shopping or something. She walked along the wide center aisle. There was so much stuff for sale!

The mall had only been on *Caesar* a few years. One day, a large trading ship had landed, spraying up a giant cloud of dust at the landing field. Everyone in Town had seen it. A very modern space trader named Sconse had met the miners. He convinced them to let him set up an automatic mall. The miners were suspicious until Sconse pulled open a big tube screen. This showed bright displays of all the marvelous stores, especially the modern hardware store. It had amazing tools and equipment, and most of them — to the miners' great surprise and delight — were for mining.

Sconse's robots built the automatic mall and stocked it, all in a day. Sconse received payment from the miners after some loud arguing over prices. He rocketed away in his spaceship. Every few months, Sconse returned. His robots kept the automatic mall repaired (the miners often damaged the advertising clowns if they got too close). And they kept it fully stocked with the latest in Galactic merchandise — especially the latest in sweets for the Great Galactic Sweetshop.

Nicky was now walking past the sweetshop. There was Sandy inside now! She waved but Sandy didn't notice. Nicky turned to go in. Then she saw that Sandy was with Fanson and...they were holding hands across the table! Nicky turned abruptly and kept walking down the big, wide aisle as if she didn't know they were there. As she left the mall, she began giggling.

Well, there was home just a short walk in front of her to the east. Beyond that, was the great utility yard. She went past her giant house. She began strolling toward the north wall of the utility yard. The north wall had an entrance gate near each end. There was one in the yard's west wall near their house. However, maybe Father or Kevin would be around the house or up on the roof.

She didn't want to be seen going in. She'd have to find another way.

Chapter 23 – Utility Yard

At the gate in the utility yard's north wall, Nicky paused and looked around to see if anyone was watching. No one was. The town-kids said no one but the miners had ever been in the utility yard. They said the miners would be angrier than ever if a kid went in. The utility yard was where all the machinery was that kept the town running, especially the Great Computer.

However, it was work-time and the miners were far away hunting for treasure. So, Nicky approached the gate to see if she could figure out how to open it and get in. She was dying to learn more about all the machinery and systems inside. The Great Computer would not tell her any of these details. She didn't have permission from the miners.

She had learned from the older town-kids that here was the location of Town's electricity, water, computer control, and other services. All except sewage and trash processing. These were a short distance northeast away from the utility yard, because they were so messy and smelly. Most of the miners didn't care how anything smelled, but this was how the building company that had built Town sixteen years ago did things. Robots mostly took care of all the machinery and equipment in the utility yard. Now and then, miners like Flart, who liked working with machines, would come to the utility yard just to check things out in person.

Nicky didn't know this and thought no one ever entered. She thought that if she could, she'd have it all to herself.

When the serving robot had brought their drinks, Sandy and Fanson had reached for them at the same time. Their hands accidentally touched. Fanson paused. It was the first time he'd ever touched her. He looked over at her. She lifted her drink and began to enjoy it, as if nothing had happened. But he felt like something special had just happened. She wasn't like the other older town girls. She was so different! She talked of so many amazing things. She was so smart. And fearless! She seemed not afraid of anything. *A girl.*

He loved being around her. It made him feel happy. And the closer he got to her, the happier he felt. What an amazing thing!

Now she was asking him what he thought about her sermon thing, that long talk she'd just made that everyone around Town had heard. He had felt his ears burning with embarrassment when she'd done that. He thought for sure the other kids would all turn and point to him and start laughing. He was so glad his father and all the miners were gone. That may have made them mad. They were hard to predict sometimes... But the other kids had all come to a stop in what they were doing and listened curiously. Then, when she had finished, they all started playing again as if nothing had happened.

Fanson tried hard to think of something to say about her sermon that would impress her. But, as usual, she had spoken much faster than he could listen. He thought of something. Looking away, he said, "Um, I was just thinking that I would like to meet Jesus sometime. Is he on a nearby world?" Then he got excited and suddenly said: "Imagine if we flew off in a spaceship to meet him!"

He looked at her and saw that this had amused her. He also noticed that her hand was resting on the table next to her glass. He reached forward and held her hand. When she didn't jerk back or yell or anything, he began breathing again. Her eyebrows were way up again. No one he knew could make their eyebrows go up as high as Sandy! But he was holding her hand, and now felt like he was in another world. She sipped her drink using her other hand. She began explaining to him that you didn't need a spaceship to meet Jesus.

The gate to the utility yard was as high as the wall. It was actually made of the same material. She had to get the Great Computer to unlock it for her. Again, Nicky talked the Great Computer into giving her more permission than the miners had first given. This was just as she had done at the sand buggies. She really had a knack for this. Nicky smiled when she heard a loud click. The gate slid open for her.

Computers that understood speech were very smart. However, they understood things only in an exact way. They were not very clever. On modern worlds, special lawyer-engineers had to be hired to instruct the computers in permissions and security matters. Otherwise, clever criminals could hack into the computer. Nicky was fond of the magazine: *The Galactic Hacker*. The magazine talked about all the latest ways hackers were getting into computers, and how to protect against them. Nicky was fascinated by all the different software tools hackers used to break in. There were the simple, old-fashioned ways: viruses, worms, Trojan horses. And there were the professional ways, usually used by groups at war with each other. These were software soldiers from just one to whole armies, software torpedoes, network missiles, and software battleships containing all the others and protected by a 'hull' made of normal software.

Nicky saw inside the utility yard for the first time. She again looked back outside to see if anyone was watching. What was that! Around the far corner she thought she'd seen someone suddenly pull back. Her eyes grew very big as she watched the corner for a while longer. Her heart began thumping strongly. Finally, she let out her breath that she'd been holding. She told herself that it was her imagination; she was just overly excited. She looked around quickly, stepped through the gate, and told the Great Computer to close it fast.

She was at last in the utility yard! She clasped her hands together and hopped up and down in excitement. She had already seen all the fascinating buildings, structures, and equipment around her from high atop the roof of her house. And now she was up close to it all. She went walking around at random. There was strange, manmade gravel under her feet that went 'crunch, crunch, crunch' as she walked. She heard no one else. And she saw none of the robots. The miners always had them busy doing other things.

Everywhere — to her great delight — there were little cards attached to everything, describing what the device was or what the building was for. The buildings were old looking. They'd been there since the beginning of Town. Nicky also asked the Great Computer lots of questions through her wrist computer. To her joy, she found the building with the Great Computer in it. But it would not let her in. It was sealed off. It would only open if something were seriously wrong with it. And then only to a repairman.

Nicky suddenly thought she'd heard something. She paused to listen. Hearing nothing more, she continued looking all around.

Sandy finished her Stellar Splatter Matter and set the glass down with a bump. She said it was time to go. But Fanson wanted to stay. He reached for her hand. She pulled it away. He was acting unusual, Sandy thought to herself. And he kept staring at her. But she liked him and didn't mind. He was the only other teenager on the planet.

"Keep talking about stuff," he said to her.

But Sandy was talked out. "You talk for a while. You're too quiet, anyway." She waited for him to speak.

Fanson stammered around a little, trying to think of what to say. Then he suddenly grinned his wide grin. He looked around quickly to make sure they were still alone. He leaned forward. "Want to hear a secret?"

Sandy's eyebrows shot up. She leaned back. "I'm not sure. What is it?"

"Well, you've got to promise not to tell."

Sandy's face wrinkled up with a distasteful look.

Fanson quickly said: "It's nothing bad! I just don't want it to get out. Promise, okay?" He reached forward and held her hand.

"Well, okay," Sandy heard herself saying.

Fanson suddenly sat straight up and grabbed the edges of the table. He looked very proud of himself. Then he leaned forward again. "When I clean Father's mining stuff, sometimes I find little bits of treasure! I've been keeping it in a safe place. And someday I'm going to buy a spaceship and be a space trader!"

All of a sudden, Fanson became very talkative and excited. Sandy had never seen him this way before. Before she could scold him for stealing, the boy began telling her everything he planned to do. He told her about all the worlds he would visit with his spaceship and everything he'd buy. He might even buy a whole world someday!

In spite of herself, she had grown excited listening. She even forgot to scold him.

Then he looked straight at Sandy and put both of his hands on hers. He leaned forward and said quietly, his voice shaking a little: "I want you to go with me, Sandy."

Sandy's eyebrows rose up higher than they'd ever gone up. She cleared her thoughts and said, "Ummm. Let me think about this. And it's time for us to go."

They both rose to go. She said, "You need to get back to school...where you can learn more about spaceships." She grinned at him, and he beamed back at her. "And I have some Bible study I need to go do..."

The waiter robot came up, and Fanson, true to his word, paid.

They left the automatic mall. Fanson insisted on walking her home before he went back to school. All the way, he kept walking up closer and closer to Sandy until he was brushing against her. Sandy would then step away, or suddenly drop back and walk on his other side. So, their path back, if it were drawn on a map, would have been quite zigzagged back and forth. They reached her door...

Nicky was having the time of her life wandering all around the utility yard. She passed the humming nuclear electrical generators, the gurgling water pumping stations, and the other facilities that supplied all the houses of Town.

There was more than one of everything. If anything broke down, a spare was needed right away. The nearest world selling spare parts was far away.

Nicky heard a sound again. She looked around a corner. One of the other gates to the utility yard was open! Her eyes grew big. This wasn't good. She crept closer to see why.

There stood three miners! But it was work-time. They should have been out mining. She thought she recognized two of them: Mr. Folor and Mr. Fearbiter. Hadn't they been two of the miners that had tried to take Kevin's pink stone away from him? She didn't recognize the third.

They walked over and closed the gate. Then, they looked around. Nicky was behind some chemical processing equipment with lots of tubes. She didn't think they could see her.

The three miners began talking about something. They seemed excited. One would say something then end it with a serious belch, as the miners always did. Another would say something else and then belch, too. They began swinging their arms with wild gestures. When their voices and belching grew too loud, the one she didn't recognize shushed them down.

Nicky was dying of curiosity to know what they were talking about and who the third miner was. She quietly crept even closer. She had to move so slowly. She was getting so close that they might hear the crunching gravel under her feet.

She thought about asking their children later. They would know which miners had returned early from treasure hunting. However, she was too impatient. Nicky held her wrist computer up to her mouth. Whispering, she told the Great Computer to listen to the voices and tell her who they were. But Nicky had not told the computer to whisper. The computer's voice spoke out: "Miners Fearbiter, Folor, and Fykrier."

All three miners suddenly looked over in her direction. One let out a loud belch. Nicky ducked down so they couldn't see her. But then she began hearing loud crunch, crunching sounds as the three miners began stumping over toward her.

Nicky whirled around and scurried off in the other direction. She heard a shout from behind. One of them had seen her. She was really in trouble now!

She ran between two buildings. When she popped out the other side, she thought she had gotten away. She looked for the nearest gate. Crunch, crunch! Around the corner came one of the miners. He roared angrily and dashed toward Nicky, his arms stretched out to grab her.

Nicky yelped and ran across the pathway. She got away by squirming through a pile of equipment. She came out the other side. She heard another miner nearby! She ran behind a building. They were so close! Off she ran again.

Nicky kept hiding behind buildings and running between piles of equipment and supplies. The three miners chased her throughout the yard. They spread out, trying to surround her. But Nicky was fast as a mouse and kept getting away.

Now she'd lost her way and didn't know which way any of the gates were. She hid in the dark corner of an equipment shed. She still heard the miners crunching around and calling out to each other in angry voices. She gulped, and began to pray, begging the Lord to deliver her from this awful situation.

Sandy had been trying to talk Fanson into going to school and leaving her alone. But he wanted to follow her into her house. She stood blocking the doorway. He said he wanted to help her do her Bible study. But she was uncomfortable with how excited and weird he was behaving.

Finally, Sandy had had enough. She stood straight up, her eyes flashing with disapproval. This always made her seem to tower almost a foot taller. She pointed to the school and told Fanson to "Get!"

Fanson looked up at her as if seeing her for the first time. Why was she now telling him to go away? He couldn't figure it out. He began to feel awful. He began to feel hurt. Somehow, he'd really messed things up. He could hear his father's voice in his mind, yelling at him whenever he wasn't cleaning something just perfectly. Fanson frowned. She wasn't taking him seriously. He'd have to prove himself to her.

"Sandy, I'll show you!" He pointed a finger at her. "I mean what I say, and I'll *show* you!" He whirled around and marched away, and not in the direction of school. He shouted over his shoulder, "You'll just see, Sandy!"

She was holding her hand to her mouth. She felt very upset that the boy was suddenly so angry. She hadn't meant to anger him. She just wanted him to go away.

Then Sandy saw him turn around suddenly. Now he looked sad. He slowly put his hands out in front of him, as if pleading with her. Then just as suddenly, he spun around and stormed away.

Sandy closed the door. She couldn't figure him out. She would go ask Father. No! That suddenly felt quite uncomfortable. Hmph. She'd always been able to talk to Father about everything before. Not this time, though.

She went to look for Nicky but couldn't find her or even Kevin.

Nicky had had an idea. She was speaking to her wrist computer. She was making it draw a map on its screen of the utility yard. She told the Great Computer to show dots for the three miners chasing her. It knew where they were by the direction of their voices. She wished there were video cameras. But the miners wouldn't allow them anywhere in Town. Miners would hate being watched by other miners who might see how to get in to their treasure chambers.

Nicky didn't have much time. The miners were getting closer. She could hear them! She watched the map closely. She could see exactly where the miners were now. She saw a break between them! She crept out and scurried toward it.

Using the map on her wrist computer, she was keeping away from them. But just barely. It was like a game of cat and mouse. It kept going on and on. She would find some place to hide and wait there while they searched and searched. When one of them got close, she ran the other way.

She just couldn't seem to work her way toward one of the gates. It was as if the miners were keeping in the way. How long would they keep this up? Why wouldn't they just give up and go away? And why weren't they out mining today, of all days??

The chase went on. But Nicky would not be caught. Her clothes were damp. She was sweating like crazy. If only there was someone to help her. Over and over she scrambled away from them, found a hiding place, and prayed to the Lord.

Finally, she saw on her map one of the chasing miners moving away in an odd direction. Now things were better. Back and forth she went, getting farther away from the other two. Finally, she made it to the southwest gate!

She told the Great Computer to open it for her, and it did. The computer was still completely fooled about her permission. As soon as the gate had opened enough, she slipped through and told it to close.

Where to go?! If the miners were still chasing her, she didn't want to lead them to her house. She couldn't see the miners on the map anymore because the wall blocked their voices and sounds. Where to hide then? She peeked around the corner of the utility yard wall. The sand buggies! Lots of places to hide. She ran over.

She was about to climb into one of the larger ones, when a head suddenly popped up in front of her. Nicky yelped and fell over backwards, landing in the sand on her rear end.

There was a silly laugh. It was Kevin!

"Nicky! Help me get this sand buggy working, I want to get out of here. Flydeckerson's after me. He and his gang want to kill me for getting them in trouble!"

Before Nicky could speak, she heard something. She looked behind the sand buggies. One of the miners was coming around the far southeast corner of the utility yard. He shook his fist, yelled, and began running.

Nicky scrambled to her feet and jumped into the buggy, knocking poor Kevin over and down to the floor. She began talking desperately to her wrist computer and madly tapping codes at the buggy's dashboard. Lights came on all over the dash board as the buggy came to life. Nicky jerked the control stick and the buggy jumped to begin moving. Kevin had just gotten to his feet and was now tossed backwards. He bounced on the seat and right over it. He fell into the vehicles bed in the back.

Nicky jerked the control stick wildly as she drove the buggy out from the other buggies. The miner, Fykrier, was almost to them. He was yelling at them to stop or he'd clobber them.

Kevin was in the back rolling back and forth. Nicky had the buggy twisting and turning. Kevin felt his legs drop away as he began to slide out the back of the buggy. Its tail gate was down. Kevin looked around and shrieked in terror to see the large, ugly face of the miner. Big, hairy arms were reaching toward him. He grabbed for the edge of the buggy's bed.

The miner almost had Kevin. Then, the buggy stopped for an instant and began pivoting. This let Kevin quickly get his legs under him. He sprang from the ground up to the bed, leaving the miner grabbing empty air. The miner stumbled and reached for the buggy, which quickly began moving away. He missed and fell to the ground with a crash and a big puff of dust. He cursed awfully, shook his fists at them, and let out a loud, angry belch.

Nicky slammed the control stick down and the buggy shot forward now with nothing in its way.

Kevin was holding tightly to the edge of the buggy's side. He felt the wind begin blowing his hair as Nicky raced the buggy forward. Kevin began creeping quickly forward. He glanced behind to see the miner getting to his feet and going to another buggy.

Kevin reached the front seat just as Nicky pulled the buggy up to Port Gate. She quickly tapped the code and opened the gate. They tore out of Town and away, the gate closing behind.

Nicky shouted: "Where should we go?! Where should we go?!"

"I know! I know!" Kevin cried. "Give me the stick!"

Nicky let him shove her out of the way and take over piloting the fast-moving buggy. She looked back toward Port Gate in worry.

Kevin drove them out behind the hills surrounding the landing field.

Chapter 24 – Miners

It was a peaceful Sunday back at their house. Sandy had spent the longest time wandering around the garden. She had just entered Father's study on the first floor to talk to him about something important.

Suddenly, there was a loud pounding at their door. It was Noon. Sandy thought that it must be Fanson, come back for lunch.

Father went to see who it was with Sandy behind him. As soon as he unlocked the door, it kicked open. There was a group of angry miners, Mr. Fan out in front. He demanded to know where his treasure was. There was loud yelling. Someone yelled something about a treasure chamber being broken into.

Just then, Fearbiter and Folor arrived. They were yelling something about the missionary kids breaking into the utility yard.

Then a sand buggy drove up and loudly slid to a stop. The miner in it shouted that the missionary kids had just escaped out Port Gate in a stolen sand buggy. They'd broken the gate and it wouldn't open!

The miners reached in and grabbed the poor missionary and his daughter. They roughly led them off toward the meeting hall at the center of Town — where only miners had ever gone before...

Kevin told Nicky that he knew where they could hide. He pulled the buggy to a stop beside an outcropping of rocks. He told her there was a tunnel down to the great chambers underground. He said the foofs would help them. They were his friends.

Nicky looked at him in shock. "Kevin, that's just a dream that you had! There's no foofs or tunnel or anything!"

"Yes, there is!" He jumped out of the buggy, ran through the rocks to where the tunnel should be...

And found only sand. It was just as it had been when he had first found it; before falling in.

Nicky came up behind him. "There's nothing here." She grabbed his arm and began pulling him back toward the buggy. "We've got to get out of here!"

"NO!" he howled. He jerked away from her, and then ran in the opposite direction.

"Kevin, come back here! They're after us! We have to get away." Nicky chased after him.

As he slipped between the rocks to get away from his older sister, Kevin began sobbing. It had all been a dream after all! There were no foofs, no tunnel.

He stepped out of the other side of the rocks. He didn't feel like running anymore anyway.

Nicky caught up and grabbed him firmly. "Come on, Kevin," she said. "Let's get back around to the buggy!"

They turned to walk back around the rocks to the buggy. Kevin gasped and pointed. "Nicky, look!"

There in the sand at their feet was a familiar flat rock. There were little control pebbles here and there near the edge. But what was most amazing was that something was written on the rock in large letters: Kevin's name!

Kevin jumped onto the rock. It bounced up and down a little because there was nothing under it. "Come on, Nicky. I know how to work this thing. Let's go see if the foofs will help us!"

To continue reading, get MISSIONARY KIDS ON TREASURE WORLD – PART 2 on Amazon.com…